Grave Intentions

Nazri Noor

GRAVE INTENTIONS

First edition. October 21, 2018.

Copyright © 2018 Nazri Noor.

ISBN: 978-1-7288-0728-7

Chapter 1

The world looks so different upside down. Try it. Hang off the side of your bed, then stare at something. But don't do it for too long or the blood rushes to your head, doing funny things to your mind and your vision. You have the luxury of setting yourself upright.

I didn't. This bald dude who was clearly a fan of protein shakes and leather jackets had me dangling by the ankle. Sad story, really. All I wanted was a burger, and the Happy Cow was closing soon, so I shadowstepped, took a back alley, then wham! I ran into mustachioed Mr. Clean and his death-grip of a hand.

Hi. My name is Dustin Graves, and I'm in trouble.

The attacker – let's call him Meathead – was the schoolyard bully, and I was the scrawny kid with all the lunch money. The way he had me completely at his mercy shouldn't have been physically possible. It was effortless, how he held me up with one hand locked like a manacle around my foot.

"Is there some way I can help you?" I huffed.

The man responded by shaking me. Trust me, not the greatest feeling. All the blood pooled in my head started sloshing around, and the dimly lit alley swam in my vision. I was going to have such a headache, damn it.

"Buddy," I said. "Ouch. Seriously."

I was still trying to size him up. Definitely supernatural. Way, way too strong to be a normal. Maybe a troll with a glamour cast over him? But where would a troll even find a camouflage spell? Those beady little eyes didn't seem very intelligent. They were mad, though. That, I can tell you. Dude looked pretty upset.

He shook me again. Something fell past my ear and tinkled as it hit the ground. Loose change, I hoped. Times like these, I thought back to Vanitas and how life was easier, and more fun with him around. I had someone to talk to, and someone to count on for slicing up bad dudes and thugs, like Meathead here. But Vanitas was gone. How things had changed.

I studied my options while Meathead toed at the detritus on the ground, examining whatever he'd gotten out of my pockets by shaking me down like a coconut tree. There weren't many possibilities for me, frankly, and I needed to wrestle my way out of my attacker's grasp before my blood or my brain found its way out of my nostrils and dribbled to the floor.

Is that what happens? Hell if I know, I'm not a doctor. Worse, he could have dropped me on the concrete and split my head open. And where would that leave us? Me, snuffed out in a decidedly unglamorous fashion, and you with nothing left to read about poor, handsome, dead old Dustin Graves.

Hmm. But maybe I wanted him to drop me on my head.

"Hey buddy," I grumbled. "Buddy, come on, you keep jiggling me like that and my brain's gonna fall out of my ears. What do you want? Money? A puppy? A hug? You look like you could use a hug. Or how about a burger? Let's go for a burger. I know a place."

I yelped when the man's fingers tightened around my ankle. In my head I saw an X-ray of my foot with all the bones in it splintering. Maybe smart-ass wasn't the best approach.

"Looking for Diaz's gem," the man said. Finally, some words. He had a voice like gravel, if gravel smoked cigarettes and had a terrible whiskey habit.

"Okay," I said, trying to make my voice a little cheerier, a bit friendlier. "First off, I don't know

NAZRI NOOR

any Diaz, and second, I don't know what you mean about any gems."

I cried out when the man squeezed even harder, and I swear that time I heard something crack and splinter. I bit back the tears forming in my throat. Big boy, I told myself. Be a big boy, even if it feels like the bridge troll in human clothing just shattered your entire foot.

"I swear," I said, in my calmest voice. "I don't know what you're talking about."

Silence. I breathed in careful sips and winced, waiting for the man to crush my bones to powder, when he started to speak again, his voice rolling like distant thunder.

"Then we go to Diaz," he said.

Now, I hear you. At that point anyone sensible would have agreed on pain of losing an entire foot. For all I knew Diaz was a perfectly lovely person who just wanted to drink tea out of pretty little cups and ask me some very nice questions. But being sensible clearly isn't my defining trait. You and I wouldn't be here if that was the case.

"Nice shoes," I said.

"Huh?" Meathead looked down at his foot, which was already smoldering from the tiny little ember I had stealthily dropped onto his sock. His eyes went huge, and he started stamping out of shock. I concentrated on the ethers, on the little fibers of the sock sheathed over his other foot, and how it would be so nice of them if they too decided to go warm and toasty, and burst into

4

flames. And so they did.

Meathead did a weird little dance, hopping from one shoe to the other, which had the effect of jostling my brain around the inside of my skull. I clamped down and focused, waiting for my opening, and when it was clear that my assailant was no longer looking, I reared my free foot back and kicked the shit out of his jaw.

Not the most elegant of attacks, but the man yowled, stomping his feet and clutching his chin, and dropping me in the process. And as I fell, I held my breath. If I got the timing wrong I'd break my head open like a raw egg. But if I aimed my fall into the pool of shadow beneath me on the asphalt, if I peeled away the veil of our reality, knocked on the door of that old, familiar dimension –

Ah. Cold, and quiet, and filled with gloomy, shapeless mist. I was back in the Dark Room, and never happier to be ambling about in that bizarre, terrible realm. It was odd, perhaps, to continue thinking of my ability as shadowstepping, chiefly because I'd learned to enter the shadows with any part of my body. I guess the bit about moving through the Dark Room on my actual feet still counts, but I digress.

I wanted to reappear just at the end of the alley, at a point where I could still see. Sure, I was more confident about my abilities the more I learned to control them under Carver's tutelage, but I wasn't about to shadowstep blind to a further destination. What if I appeared in oncoming traffic?

The shadows of the Dark Room dissipated, and I emerged in the relatively warmer clime of the alley. I looked around, and hah. Perfect. I'd escaped my attacker.

Then something slammed into me with the force of a speeding car, pounding me against the alley's brick wall. The pain crashed across my back like boiling water, and maybe I heard something crack. I saw stars, and in the back of my mind, I couldn't help wondering if oncoming traffic would have been a more merciful way to break every bone in my body.

My vision swam back into focus as I struggled against the pressure bearing down against my neck. The pressure turned out to be Meathead's entire hand wrapped around my throat like a grappling hook made out of solid, frozen beef. Huh. Cold skin. To further express that he wasn't fucking around, Meathead bared his teeth. Correction. Fangs. I should have guessed he was a vampire.

Why didn't I just set him on fire, you ask? Hey, baby steps. I couldn't actually throw fireballs yet, so I improvised like I always did, by starting smaller flames, or sneaking little embers where I could put them. Still, the urge to burn rose in me again as I squirmed in his grasp. Carver once told me that an easy way to quickly diffuse a situation was to set someone's hair on fire. But this guy was totally bald.

So I focused on his eyelashes.

"You burned my shoes."

I blinked, distracted. "Sorry?" I looked down at his feet. His footwear was still mostly intact, but the bits around his ankles were somewhat blackened, the ends of his jeans singed. "Hey, let me make it up to you. If you don't snap my head off, I'll buy you some new kicks."

His lips drew back further, exposing the full length of his fangs. I should have been more terrified, but something about those chompers was so familiar. Maybe spending time with Sterling had desensitized me. But Meathead bent closer, and all numbness washed away when I saw his fangs from up close, shining wet and white in the streetlight.

"Can't replace them," he muttered. "I took these off a dead man."

I swallowed thickly. "What about a trade? My shoes for – "

"Diaz's jewel. That's what I need." His eyes cast downward to look at my feet regardless, and for a brief second I thought I had a chance of trading my shoes for my life. "Plus those are hideous."

I squirmed, taken aback. "How dare you, sir. I paid twelve whole dollars for these."

"Salimah. He's trying to be cute."

Something – someone, rather, stepped out of the shadows. Long tumbles of black hair, skin deep and dusky, lips painted blood-red. She wore a tight leather jacket, and equally tight jeans. What's with vampires and leather, seriously? Valero could get chilly at night, sure, but what was wrong with a sensible hoodie, or a nice, fuzzy sweater every now and then? Of course, vampires weren't affected by the weather, so none of it mattered. Weird perk for people who could be obliterated by sunlight.

The woman called Salimah watched me with a cool, cautious gaze, her arms folded across her chest. She raised her hand, spreading her fingers out, examining finely polished nails that were also painted blood-red. In ways, she reminded me of Layla, a succubus who had once sucked out part of my soul through a terrifyingly sexy and sexily terrifying kiss. But Salimah opened her mouth to speak, and from her fangs I could tell that she was the kind of supernatural creature who didn't deal in souls. A bloodsucker through and through.

"On any other day, Mr. Graves," she said, "I would find your cheeky banter amusing. Tonight, however, my patience is short. If you do not start giving us straight answers, my colleague here will be more than happy to rearrange your face."

I gasped. "Not my face." Seriously, though. Never the face.

The bald man growled. "Salimah, I swear."

"Okay, okay, I promise I'll stop being an asshole." I threw my hands up, the universal gesture of placation. "Like I told your buddy here, I've never heard of Diaz, and I've never heard of a jewel."

Salimah's eyebrow, shaped very much like a scimitar, raised in a sharp curve. "Then why was a man who looked exactly like you prowling around Nirvana? Why is the Heartstopper missing?"

"Nirvana? And why is the Heartstopper – look, lady, now you're just making up words. I don't know about no jewel, and I sure as hell haven't heard of any Heartstopper. What is it, like an artifact?"

Salimah stared and said nothing. After a tense few seconds, she spoke again.

"Connor. Break one of his fingers."

Meathead – Connor – smiled wide, far wider than I'd seen him smile all night. I yelped.

"Wait. Wait. What can I do to prove that I wasn't the guy who stole your whatever it was? What if I – what if I helped you find it?"

Salimah tilted her head, her lips pursed as she considered my proposal. As if I needed to owe these two anything. I needed more vampires in my life like I needed a hole in the head.

"Connor," Salimah said.

I breathed in relief.

"Break two fingers."

I struggled harder than ever, the flesh at my throat so much colder from contact with Connor's fingers, and I turned my head, aching to see if I was casting a shadow against the wall behind me. Could I step into it if I didn't have the freedom of motion? Hell, could I possibly shadowstep away from the fingers threatening to crush my windpipe? One way to find out.

But I never did. A streak of silver crashed through the alley, slamming bodily against Connor with a horrible crack. The hand holding me by the throat whizzed away as the vampire was knocked off of me, and I crumpled to the ground, clutching my neck and wheezing for breath. My head spun, looking for where Connor had been thrown. I shouldn't have been surprised to find out who my savior was.

I grimaced. Yes, I like being alive, but no, I don't like being indebted to Sterling. God, I knew he was going to lord this one over me for days, if not weeks. Months. If I live long enough, years, but seeing as how I couldn't even set foot outside the hideout for a hamburger without being half-murdered, maybe I'd be dead sooner rather than later.

Sterling growled as he held Connor against the ground, both of his hands clenched against his collar. The best way to describe Sterling was that he was slender, the kind of guy who dressed like he was the lead in a rock band, all piercings and leather and long hair. But as lanky as he looked, there was a reason Carver kept him around. I'd seen Sterling smash through a door as if it were made out of paper.

Salimah stood over the two of them, teeth bared, her upper body pushed forward like she was on the brink of attack, but something in her posture was hesitant. Clearly the two knew each other. Either she and Sterling were evenly matched, or he was her superior. Something about age, the way it worked with mages as well: chances are, the older something is, the more capable it is of breaking your face.

"Keep your fingers off him," Sterling said, his tone even and warning. It was weird hearing him being protective over me, but hey, I was going to take what I could get.

Salimah huffed, her eyes ripping like daggers in the brief moment that she glared at me. "Does he belong to you?"

For some seconds, Sterling and I locked gazes. If he said yes, then I was off the hook, possibly, but gross. Come on. I wasn't one of his thralls. Not my kink. But what if he said no?

"He belongs to someone stronger than me," Sterling said. "You don't want to mess with that." He slammed Connor one last time against the ground, then got to his feet, scraping the dust from his knees. "What do you want with this idiot, anyway?"

"Hey," I said, but Sterling's glance told me it was best to keep my mouth shut.

"Something belonging to Diaz is missing," Salimah said. I still had no idea who this Diaz was. "And I was informed that someone who looks very much like your 'friend' here was responsible for its disappearance."

Sterling rolled his eyes. "And you two immediately resorted to violence to handle this?"

"We were only going to scare it out of him. There wasn't going to be any real violence." She gave me a longing look. "Well, maybe a quick drink."

Sterling shook his head. "No more of this shit. I work with this kid. Nothing goes through our territory without me knowing. If he says he didn't steal it, he didn't steal it."

My eyes went wide. Wow. Was Sterling actually being nice to me?

"Plus he couldn't strategize on his own if his life depended on it. He's too dumb for that."

My hero.

"We'll leave it at that for now," Salimah said. "But if he comes anywhere close to Nirvana – "

"Fine," Sterling barked. "No Nirvana, as long as you remember to course this through me next time."

Salimah bent to the ground, collecting Connor from his heap. He seemed too dazed to be interested in retaliation just then, but Salimah shot me a last lethal look as they left the alley, one that said I was dead if we ever crossed paths again.

I wasn't sure if I should thank Sterling, but it seemed the right thing to do. He was already lighting a cigarette. I scratched the back of my neck, staring down the alley after Salimah and Connor.

"I – Sterling – I guess – "

"Don't mention it," he said, looking away and blowing out a thin stream of smoke into the wind. He was doing that thing where he was deliberately turning away, one hand in his pocket, legs stood apart like he really thought he was a hero. God, what a douche.

"You're lucky I showed up when I did."

I tried not to roll my eyes. "Yeah. Lucky."

He nudged his head towards the alley's exit, already walking. "Tell me all about what happened. Diaz wouldn't have sent anyone to bother you without good reason."

"Well, I was just going for a bite to eat."

Sterling shook his head. "Story of my life."

I recounted what happened as I glanced at the time on my phone. The Happy Cow was closed.

Damn it. I just wanted a burger.

Chapter 2

"A ruby in the shape of a teardrop," Carver said. "Perhaps it is a little oddly named, as the jewel does not actually stop the heart. It preserves a newly deceased body, staving off the ravages of decomposition and rot. Quite useful for vampires, I would imagine. And necromancers. And blood witches."

So that was what the Heartstopper could do. I knew it wasn't the exact same thing, but it reminded me of how I'd once been found in a morgue. Through magical means I'd been made to appear so convincingly unliving that actual professionals had declared me dead. It was the entire reason I had to shed my former life and join the arcane underground.

Gil frowned, his eyebrows like caterpillars

across his forehead. "So it's like a magic meat locker? That's all it does? So why is this Diaz so sensitive about it going missing?"

"Vampires like their treasure, I guess?" I shrugged. "Who knows."

Sterling scoffed. "Not me. You're thinking of dragons."

Asher spoke up before I did, his mouth open. It saved me the trouble of asking what Carver was undoubtedly going to consider a stupid question. "Whoa. There are dragons?"

Against all expectation, Carver smiled and nodded politely. I kept my shock to myself. Holy shit. Dragons?

We were in the hideout. You know, that dimensional chamber that Carver created, the one that was hidden in the back kitchen of a Filipino restaurant out in the Meathook. We were sitting around the hideout's living room, because yes, we have a living room now.

I'm not one to hold a grudge, but Carver was being awful nice to Asher. Rather, he'd been super nice to Asher since the beginning, and call me crazy, but it felt like he'd gone a little sour on me. Even meaner than before, is what I'm saying.

Carver, my mentor, my employer, and possibly one of the most powerful liches in existence, had done a little sprucing up when Asher joined us. Okay, a lot of sprucing up. I got that he was super stoked to have someone with enormous magical potential to mentor — a necromancer, of all things, a wielder of some of the rarest talents to be found in the arcane world – but Carver was probably spoiling him a little.

The worst thing was that Asher didn't even have the decency to let it get to his head and start acting like a jerk. There was nothing I could hate him for. He was a good kid, maybe the effect of finally having friends after being locked away by a druidic death cult. I never did ask how long he'd been with them, exactly, but he was eighteen when we found him.

I'd assumed that it was the same main reason he'd been forced to keep his hair grown out, being shut in the same room for ages, but even months after rescuing him from the Viridian Dawn, Asher maintained his luxurious head of black locks. I approved. It suited him, admittedly. It helped him fit in with the young hipsters who littered Valero's streets.

Sterling approved, too, and it wouldn't have surprised me to learn that they shared hair tips and products. Asher got along with everyone, even Sterling, of all people. Especially Sterling, who was sprawled across the sofa. The rest of us were in armchairs, because while the sofa could clearly accommodate three people, it had been designated Sterling's perch from the day it was moved into the hideout. Sterling's like a cat that way, only meaner, and with bigger teeth.

Gil, our resident werewolf, was perfectly happy with the setup. He was especially grateful about how we had wifi now. How the hell wifi could even penetrate another dimension is an excellent question, but in the short time we spent in the Japanese sun goddess Amaterasu's domicile, I saw her searching for something on a browser on her very small and very cute smart phone.

It seemed that Carver had successfully copied whatever juju she'd mixed up to enable internet access in a magical realm. It made me wonder if there was some high speed internet service provider out there that catered specifically to the arcane market. Don't laugh, you didn't know dragons existed until a minute ago either.

And me? I was waiting for the slop in my lap that hardly passed for microwaved beef stroganoff to cool down enough so I could shove it in my face. Mama Rosa, the Filipino restaurant's proprietor, had gone home for the night, and I was too hungry to order out for a fast food burger. All we had were frozen dinners, which Asher was only too happy to eat. There was also the freezer of raw steaks that made up the bulk of Gil's diet. He was very generous about sharing them with the rest of us, but I really couldn't be bothered to cook. So frozen stroganoff it was.

Carver took a sip of his boiling hot coffee, barely flinching as the magma-hot liquid slipped past his lips. I'd warned him so many times that it wasn't how humans were built, and that he'd have to behave better if he wanted to pass for a mortal when we went out for lattes, but did he ever listen to me?

"Diaz is a blood witch," Carver said. "He has his reasons for being attached to the Heartstopper. I imagine he uses it to further his research. Perhaps he even enchanted the ruby himself."

"And I don't think it's easy for just anyone to break into Nirvana, but the culprit managed, somehow," Sterling said. He caught the befuddled look on my face. "Oh. Nirvana's like a vampire commune, and Diaz is their leader."

I stared at him, mouth agog. "That's a thing? What, like a whole nest of them?"

"Living underground. So, sort of like a cave." Sterling grinned, waggling his eyebrows. "There's more in common between dragons and vampires than you thought."

Carver set down his coffee and scoffed. "Dragon or vampire, I'd say that this is much more a matter of ownership. Wouldn't you all agree? If someone invades your home and steals something of value, you would want retribution." He turned to me with a narrowed gaze. "Especially if it's someone easily recognized, or easily found."

His stare said it all. You're both, Dustin. Both.

You know, I try not to dwell too much over the fact that I'm kind of famous – but for all the wrong reasons. Apparently very few people had heard of someone who could walk through shadows, or could summon them as bladed weapons in this reality. That was my gift, and word spread. Maybe that was how Salimah and Connor knew who to hunt down.

"But why me? You guys know I don't go around stealing shit."

"Except for that beer at the grocery the other week," Gil said, avoiding my gaze.

"Or the pack of cigarettes from behind the counter at that one gas station," Sterling said. "And I still don't know how the hell you did it, but thanks for the freebie."

"Okay, geez. Dustin has itchy fingers, I got it." They were right, too. If I wasn't on a mission, something inside me just wanted to nick stuff when it could, like a void that needed filling. "But back on topic. How the hell could someone who looks like me just walk around town stealing stuff?" My mouth fell open. "Unless – "

Carver nodded. "Thea."

My skin crawled. The mention of her name alone had that effect on me. Thea Morgana acted as my boss and mentor for as long as it benefited her, pretending to be my friend and ally. As it turned out, she was the one responsible for sacrificing me.

Some time back I thought I'd had the pleasure of killing her, by summoning just enough of the Dark Room's living shadows to spear her through her torso. We discovered, too late, that she'd escaped justice – and death – yet again.

Oh. Does that seem too extreme? Let me put it this way. If someone tries to kill you – you, specifically – and you survive, you would want revenge. You would want justice. But considering everything that Thea had done to me, I was way past justice. I wanted her gone. If that meant dead, then so be it.

I grimaced. "I hate that you're probably right. It could be Thea looking to stir shit up again. But why would she want the Heartstopper?"

"Remember that this was how they found you," Carver said. "In a state of torpor. Everyone thought you dead. It's possible that she's found some other suitable victim to sacrifice, and that she wants to repeat the process. To preserve their corporeal form, for whatever reason."

Gil leaned forward, clasping his hands together. "Listen. You say this woman was a high-ranking member of the Lorica."

He was right. For years Thea worked as a sorceress for the Lorica, the organization that governed North American magic and mages. She bade her time, masquerading as one of the good guys as she researched more ritual magic and grew in power. Thea was a highly intelligent and cunning person – if she could still be called a person – was what Gil was trying to say.

"She's not going to try the same thing twice," I said. "She's too clever for that. There's something else brewing, and I don't like it."

"Consider the possibility that she's misdirecting," Sterling said, offering a rare bit of insight. "How about that? And this is what's worse. You guys say she's good at glamours."

"She tricked us all, remember?" Carver said. "None of us could sniff her out. Her power to bend the light and cast an illusion about herself is one thing, but to evade us the way she did? The woman wields powerful enchantments."

In the form of jewelry similar to those Carver wore on his person, the amber gems adorning the rings on his fingers. It was one of those things I'd always promised I'd try to learn. Enchanting was an incredible discipline in itself. It took enormous amounts of time, effort, and magical power, but enchanted items are like the wearable tech of the arcane world. A ring that shoots fireballs, or turns you invisible, or summons burritos on command? Yes, please.

"Evasion and cloaking is one thing," Sterling said. "But infiltration is another. As long as we're sure we keep an eye on each other, and we know she can't penetrate the Boneyard? Then we're good."

I blinked. "Wait. Sorry. Did I hear you right? I think you just called this place the Boneyard."

Asher cleared his throat and reddened. "It's nice to call it something other than just 'home' or 'the hideout.' I like it. We've got a vampire, a werewolf, a lich, and I'm a necromancer." He gestured at me, smiling sheepishly. "And you use the shadows and the darkness. We're like the good bad guys. Like, the undead, but decent undead, you know?"

"Isn't that clever," Carver said, with no hint of sarcasm whatsoever.

Asher sat up, his chest puffing out as he beamed. "Sterling and I talked about it," he said. "Seemed like a good idea."

I couldn't help feeling left out.

Carver nodded, and smiled. "The Boneyard it is then."

I gritted my teeth.

We were dismissed after that, sent off to do whatever we wanted. The Heartstopper being missing didn't mean the end of the world, but this whole situation just reeked of Thea. Where she went, destruction followed. But if it really was her behind it, then how were we supposed to even track her down in the first place?

I had more questions. So many. Pressing matters I couldn't discuss with the – with the members of the Boneyard. Damn it, Asher. It did sound cool. Ugh.

I headed to my room, shut the door, and took out my phone. It didn't matter what I thought about the preferential treatment Asher was getting – we were all grateful for the gift of wifi. I looked up Herald Igarashi, then initiated a video call.

He picked up in three rings, appearing on the screen in his glasses and, from the upper half of his body that I could see, one of his typical outfits, which made him look very much like a stylish librarian. It worked out for him, anyway, the buttoned-up shirts, the ties, the vests. It looked like he was at home, for once. Guy worked too much.

A talented alchemist and a very competent sorcerer in his own right, Herald was an archivist for the Lorica. He was tasked with sorting, collecting, and cataloguing the strange and dangerous artifacts that passed through his section of the organization's extensive Gallery. He also liked to mention that he was something of an amateur demonologist, but I wasn't sure how that translated into what he did for a living, if it did at all.

"Sup," I said.

"I am not going for brunch in this damn weather, Graves. And I'm up to my ears in lobster rolls. No more."

"What? No, no, this is about something else. I needed to talk to someone who knows a lot about magic, but I can't talk to Carver."

"So you called me?" Herald straightened his posture. Flattery always worked, but hey, it was as honest as I could get without blowing smoke up his ass. Okay, too much smoke. I could tell he was restraining a grin. "Ask away."

"How much do you know about glamours?"

Herald squinted a little, then pushed up his glasses as they started to slide down his nose.

"Oh. That's really advanced stuff, Dust. I know you're chomping at the bit to learn more magic, and no offense, but you can't even launch a fireball yet. Glamours are complex illusions. Even I can't do them consistently." He passed his hand over his face, his fingers trailing little violet skeins of magic. "I can change my eye color though. See?"

He bent closer to his phone. Damn right. His eyes were blue now. "Show-off," I said, half fondly, and half in total, utter jealousy. He grinned, then blinked, and his eyes were back to brown.

"I'm curious, though. Humor me. Why are you suddenly interested in glamours? I know that Thea used a powerful one to impersonate someone long-term." He frowned, looked off-camera, then back again. "Wait. Is this about her?"

I nodded. "Looks like someone's impersonating me, or at least they did to go and steal something called the Heartstop – "

"The Heartstopper?" Herald's face was practically pressed up against his phone now.

"So you know about it."

He nodded. "Belongs to a powerful local blood witch. Used to preserve corpses. Shaped like a drop of blood. That Heartstopper, yes?"

"Exactly what Carver said."

Herald clucked his tongue. "Can't be good, dude. Whoever's behind this, Thea or no, they've got to have a very specific reason for wanting the Heartstopper. And if they're impersonating you, that's just going to get you into heaps more trouble."

I sighed. "I was kind of hoping you'd have some answers besides what Carver already told me, but here we are."

"I'm flattered, Graves, but my huge brain can only process so much. We need backup. Someone with a stronger information network." He rubbed his chin, then gave me a smile. "What are your thoughts on checking in with your eight-legged girlfriend?"

Chapter 3

"Now, normally, you can use anything to cast a circle. Maybe draw it in chalk, or even scatter a bunch of twigs in the right configuration, and you'll have something worthy of calling an entity's attention."

Asher's lips hung slightly parted as he absorbed Herald's every word. I'd casually mentioned to Carver that I was going on a communion, and asked if I could take the kid with me. The answer was a vehement "No," until I followed up and mentioned that Herald was coming. "Oh, that's fine then."

It was kind of telling that he didn't trust me to babysit Asher on my own, but was perfectly happy to allow it with someone from the Lorica on the team. Carver might have seen something in Herald that night we all had dinner together, something almost resembling admiration. Whatever it was, I gotta say, it stung just the tiniest bit that he trusted Herald more than me.

But watching Herald carefully give instructions, I began to understand exactly why. We were in the same alley Thea had once brought me for my first communion, with Arachne, the very same entity the three of us were meaning to contact.

Asher was nodding enthusiastically at basically everything Herald said, in between sips of the frosty boba drink he had in his hand. Hey, it was a hot day. We needed to pick up the reagents for Arachne's summoning, and there was this great bubble tea place in Little China called Happy Boba. Yes, the name isn't lost on me. I wouldn't be surprised to learn that they were owned by the same people as the Happy Cow.

"So again, use whatever you want to cast a circle. Personally I like to keep things convenient for myself."

Herald snapped his fingers. Violet light pulsed from his hands, gathering into threads that snaked about his feet, drawing a flawless, glowing circle on the ground. Scratch that, it was multiple concentric circles arranged in perfect geometric symmetry, with eldritch symbols inscribed in appropriate places.

Asher gasped audibly, accentuating his

wonder with a low, awe-inspired "Wow."

I did my damnedest not to look quite as gobsmacked, but it was so, so fucking cool. Yet as hard as I was trying to keep my expression neutral, Herald was clearly doing very much the same, struggling to keep the smug little smirk from crawling across his face.

"That was so awesome," Asher said. "I wish I could do that."

"Soon," Herald said, adjusting his glasses in what I interpreted as a very self-satisfied manner. "Your boss is extremely proficient. He'll show you the ropes in due time. I mean, hey, if he could teach Dustin here how to light a spark – "

"Hey. Wow. So rude. I'm still learning."

" – then surely Carver can teach you everything you need to know about becoming a proper mage. So. Now that your circle is cast, you need to have the offerings in place." He slipped a fortune cookie out of its packet, crushing it in his fist and letting the crumbs fall into the circle. "And now the part that takes getting used to."

Herald made a motion with his wrist, almost like he was unfolding an invisible butterfly knife, and then it appeared, a glowing purple blade the size and sharpness of a scalpel. Again my insides burbled with envy, until I realized that with practice, I could hone my power to weaponize the Dark Room's shadows the exact same way. In time, I told myself. A step at a time.

Herald dragged the edge of his arcane blade

across his finger. Asher winced. So did I. The blade was sharp as anything, drawing blood as soon as it made contact with Herald's skin. He squeezed his finger, letting the blood drip into the circle. It sizzled and smoked as it hit the cement. Herald began to chant.

"You also need to incant," I said to Asher softly, careful not to interrupt Herald. "It's how you communicate your intent. Doesn't really matter what you say, as long as you tell the entity through your conviction that you deserve an audience. It's like a text message."

Asher nodded eagerly, and we looked on as the little stenciled sigil in the brick wall that marked Arachne's gateway began to spin. Within seconds it expanded into a shimmering portal of gossamer and gleaming silver. Herald sucked on his finger, then pushed his fists into his hips, admiring his work.

"Everyone pile in," he said. "Time to meet Dust's girlfriend."

"Oh my God, she's not my girlfriend."

"Says you. I felt some resistance while I was incanting, but I casually mentioned that you were coming and the window of opportunity swung wide open." He waggled his eyebrows. "She likes you, Dust. It's something to keep in mind. The entities take care of their playthings."

Playthings, he said. It made my skin crawl, remembering how that seemed to be the very dynamic the Eldest maintained with their servants. Stronger, older, and far more terrible than any of the entities of earth, all I knew of the Eldest was that they were bad, bad news, and that they warped those who served them in their image, like the shrikes, the shrieking, many-tentacled minions that made up their vast cosmic army. Or Thea herself, who grew more alien and insectoid each time I had the misfortune to encounter her.

I was about to enter the portal, this counting as my second official visit to Arachne's domicile, when Asher skidded right in front of me, practically tangling his feet in his excitement to step through. He vanished among the swirling gossamer mists. I gave Herald a questioning look, but he just shrugged.

"Hey. I won't fault the kid for his enthusiasm. That's a good thing. Great foundation to build on for learning magic, and everything else there is to know about the arcane underground."

"I'm enthusiastic, too."

He gestured at the portal. "I believe you. Get in."

I sighed and walked on through, not at all relishing the feeling of the portal somehow sticking to my clothes and hair and skin. The strands of energy made it feel very much like swimming through molasses, and the act of actually moving into the spider-queen's realm was literally like walking through spiderwebs.

Herald followed not far behind, and Asher was

already gawking at the bizarre, jade-green enormity of Arachne's domicile. Great swathes of what looked like silk draped from the ceilings, moving gently in a light breeze that none of us could feel on our skin or hair.

Braziers of stone pulsed with sickly green light, the only illumination in a dimension so dark that all we could really see were the strange, silken curtains and the great stone dais where Arachne held audience. It looked very much the same as the last time I visited, though that still gave me no comfort. What was different this time was Arachne's total absence.

I elbowed Herald in the ribs. "Where is she?" I hissed.

"Beats me," Herald said, looking around cautiously, the ghoulish light reflecting on his glasses. "She responded to my summoning, which means she should be home."

"This is so cool," Asher said absently. "I love this place."

A high, feminine voice tittered from somewhere in the unseeable ceiling far above us. "I am glad to hear it."

The silks began to shiver, and out of the silence trickled the sound of things skittering, of tiny mouths and pincers chittering in excitement. I balled my fists and stilled myself: they were coming.

Out of the corners and darkest recesses of Arachne's domicile her children came pouring in their thousands and spindly millions, spiders of every shape and species crawling down the walls, over the dais, descending from the ceiling on fine strands of silk.

Among them was the great, heaving bulk of Arachne's thorax, lowering from out of the high darkness, legs as thick and long as spears wavering as they negotiated her web. She moved headfirst, her hair and her veils brushing against the ground as she reached the floor and set her body upright. Arachne's eight legs served as her throne on the dais, the slender and wickedly white pallor of her human torso gleaming an eerie green in her domicile's jade-light.

"Herald Igarashi of the Lorica," Arachne said, her head giving the slightest nod. She turned to me, the sharpness of her smile visible under the hem of her veil. "And my sweetling, the boy who walks through shadows." Arachne tilted her head as she turned her attention towards Asher. "This one I do not know."

"Asher Mayhew," he said eagerly, one hand still wrapped around his extra large boba, the other holding out a plastic bag full of fortune cookies. "And here you go, ma'am." He walked directly for her, approaching the dais without invitation or regard for etiquette. I would have panicked and said something if Arachne hadn't laughed first.

"This one is so precocious, and trusting. How very sweet."

Asher beamed widely. The fucker wasn't afraid in the slightest, not of Arachne, and not of the millions of her young carpeting the walls and the floor. She turned towards me again, her grin a little sharper, a little eviler this time. "Perhaps I have found myself a new sweetling."

I groaned. "Oh, come on. Not you too."

Asher cocked his head, alarmed. "Sorry, what was that? What do you mean?"

I shook my head. "It's nothing," I said, just as one of Arachne's legs darted out to collect the plastic bag from Asher's outstretched hand. The huge bristles and pincer at the end of her legs brushed against Asher's skin as she took away the cookies. He hardly flinched, still looking at me questioningly. The kid was either really dumb, or really brave, or both.

"It's his first communion, Arachne," I said. "We hope you find it acceptable that we've brought him along, to learn how to commune by starting with one of the kindest, most gracious entities I know."

Somewhere behind me I swear Herald snorted. Asher kept slurping his boba. But Arachne smiled. Sometimes, depending on the entity, a different approach was needed to grease the wheels, but with almost all that I'd encountered, flattery was the choicest way to go.

"No harm done, Dustin Graves. And we see that he is indeed very enthusiastic about his learnings in the arcane. You are free to visit

Arachne's domicile whenever you wish, Asher Mayhew." Her veils and all the silks in the chamber rustled when she tittered again, laughing softly with one hand over her mouth. "He's certainly dealing with this new reality far better than you did when we first met, sweetling. Do you recall? In the words of your people I believe that you were, oh, how do you say it. Shitting your pants?"

"What?" I blustered, and thanked the light of her domicile for disguising the fact that my cheeks had gone searing red. "That's ridiculous. I mean I – "

Arachne held up one hand, the length of her arm glittering with the myriad jewels and trinkets she wore. "Enough pleasantries. Tell me what you need." With her other hand she was already riffling through the plastic bag, as if to select the best of the fortune cookies out of an assortment that, naturally, all looked exactly the same.

"Information," Herald said, with a brief bow of his head. "As we all know is your specialty, Arachne."

She grinned. "How very correct." She smashed a fortune cookie with one fist, dug out the little slip of paper with the fortune on it, then read it, chuckling. "This says that I will be lucky in love. How droll." She crammed the entire mess – cookie, wrapper, fortune – in her mouth, chewing aggressively as shards and splinters of the little treat erupted from between her fangs. "And what do you need to know?"

"My father," I blurted out. Herald fixed me with a look, but said nothing. "I asked you once if you could help me find him."

"Ah. Of course."

Arachne probed at the air around her, as if looking for something. Then, pinching at some seemingly invisible object with her thumb and forefinger, she tugged. In the light I could just barely make out the sheen of a strand of spider silk.

There must have been dozens, hundreds around her, each attached to one of the secret-finding spiders she kept under her employ, their tethers hanging around her invisibly until she needed them. She pulled on it again, like it was the rope of a small, delicate dinner bell. "Give my offspring time. They will come with what we need soon enough."

"There's another thing," Herald said.

"Oh. Is there?"

I nodded. "We have reason to suspect that my old mentor is masquerading as me somehow. Using a glamour, maybe, or one of her enchantments. She was found stealing an artifact."

Arachne pressed a long, taloned finger against the side of her temple, turning it like a screw. "How curious. Why would that be necessary? Why would she not simply take what she needed?"

Herald lifted a hand in agreement. "See, exactly. That's why we're here. We need your wisdom, and access to your network. Tell us what you can find, why this woman is impersonating Dustin. It seems so pointless."

"Hey."

"He's so insignificant."

"Seriously, Herald."

"Now this," Arachne said, a hand on her chin. "This demand is more complex. What would you have to offer in return, I wonder?"

Herald and I watched each other cautiously. "We need her help," he muttered. "Your friends might have ways, but nothing like what she can do."

Arachne stretched her neck out and spoke louder. "Is that a 'Yes,' sweetling?"

I chewed my lip and eyed her carefully. "What would we have to give in return, Arachne?"

"Oh, such trifling matters can be discussed at a later date." She grinned widely, her teeth like perfect chips of malachite. "If you had asked for something smaller, I would have continued to offer my aid. But this is quite a demand. For now, consider it my last gift. A final favor. But no more. From this point on, anything you ask of me or my brood will involve payment more expensive than, say, a handful of fortune cookies."

She laughed again, one hand over her mouth, the other waving dismissively, as if she had practiced this very gesture in the past. It looked like she was pantomiming, trying to be human. Technically, Arachne was human once. Still, it felt too measured, too deliberate. She seemed to be trying to put us at ease, but it only made me that much more apprehensive.

Asher was switching his gaze rapidly between the three of us, the fat, huge straw of his tea drink still stuffed in his maw. He wouldn't have looked out of place with a bag of popcorn in his hand, really. He might have been new to this, but even he could sense the potential severity of Arachne's payment.

"Dude," Herald said softly. "She's given you enough freebies as it is. This is your investment. Whatever she demands from now on, that's Future Dustin's problem. Sure as hell beats being attacked by vampires every night. Do it."

I stared at Arachne resolutely. This wasn't about burgers. Someone out there had stolen my identity. Someone was wearing my face. And if it was Thea, then we needed some way to find her, so I could put something sharp into her heart and stop her fucking our lives up, once and for all.

I nodded.

Arachne clapped her hands together and squealed. She was far, far too happy about this. "Excellent, sweetling." She raised her head, then cooed. "And what timing, too. Here comes my offspring to deliver what she's discovered of your father."

One of Arachne's secret-spiders descended from the ceiling, its strand of web so fine that it looked like it was floating towards me. On its back was a bright blue gem. Through some form of magic, these bejeweled spiders were connected to Arachne with bonds even stronger than her regular children, making it so they could flawlessly store and convey information to their many-legged mother. It made her a fantastic resource for intelligence, and possibly a very terrible enemy to have.

I held out my hand as the spider descended, and when it was only feet away I noticed that it had its legs wrapped around something glimmering. A gem? What the – no. It was the plastic wrapper of a fortune cookie, the same brand that we always brought Arachne.

The spider landed gently in my palm, deposited the fortune cookie, then ascended into the ceiling once again, the sapphire on its back turning into a bright blue speck as it disappeared into the darkness.

"A cookie?" I said, hoping that my confused expression wouldn't offend Arachne.

"With information on your father," she said, her head raised with confidence and, I thought, what looked like triumph.

I knew these entities were crazy. Who knew why these gods and demons and mythological creatures wanted to be so obtuse about everything, but hey, they came from a different time. There was no sudoku to pass the time and shit, no porn, so it was all about the riddles.

This all grumbled inside of my head as I unwrapped the fortune cookie, then split it in half. I pulled out the tiny scroll of paper, unfurled it, and read the words printed there. I couldn't help myself. My mouth fell open.

"What is it?" Asher asked, his mouth a perfect, dumbstruck mirror of my own.

"An address. It's my dad's address."

Chapter 4

Herald's face scrunched with every passing second, driven slowly to annoyance and insanity by every tiny slurping sound.

"Asher. Seriously. Aren't you done with that stupid thing?"

Asher stopped chewing, swallowed thickly, then gave him a wide-eyed look. "I wouldn't want to waste it. Come on, dude. Lemme finish my drink."

Herald bared his teeth. It was kind of amusing seeing him get so worked up over something so dumb, but that was part of being friends with Igarashi. He was so chill, and calm, and level-headed, until he wasn't.

"They're tapioca balls, for God's sake. Just throw the damn thing out. Surely that lich boss of yours pays you enough that you don't have to scrimp and save on every little thing."

I chuckled. "Let him be, Herald. You try being locked up in a room for years. Everything's new to him, so it's a fun experience. Right, Asher?"

Grateful, I suppose, for the little defense, Asher gave me a small smile. I was the one who suggested we try out some boba – which he clearly loved, quite unlike kombucha, which he spat out on first contact. We were on a park bench not far from the alley where Arachne's sigil was tethered. She'd let us go after handing me my father's actual, physical new home address inside of a fortune cookie.

We were in Heinsite Park, specifically. It was the same place I'd been abducted for my ritual murder, the same place I first met Sterling and Gil the night they tried to kidnap me, and the same place I discovered that I could finally cast a spell by lighting a vampire on fire. Good times, good memories.

Asher had been sucking on his boba tea the entire time, astoundingly unbothered as he was by both Arachne's appearance and that of her offspring, something which was clearly driving Herald to the brink of madness. With a last, exaggerated slurp, Asher hoovered up the rest of the tapioca balls, crumpled up his empty cup, then tossed it in the garbage.

"There. I'm done. No need to be so pissy about it."

Herald gritted his teeth. Asher reached his hand out towards me, palm open, and I handed him the little slip of paper with the address on it. He clearly didn't know enough of the outside world to do anything with that information, but his specific portfolio of arcane power meant that he had a way of sniffing out life energy.

It was extremely limited in range, a severely watered-down version of what the Lorica's Eyes could do with their scrying, but the extent of his ability was really all I needed. I just wanted him to reach out and sense if my dad was okay.

Asher closed his fingers around the fortune, his eyes shutting gently. A faint mantle of green energy began to pulse around his closed fist. The fact that he needed to actually handle the slip of paper told me that he had, in addition to the strange range of abilities necromancers possessed, access to a kind of psychometry. He required an object attached to the person in question, and the rest, pardon the expression, was magic.

The green light cloaking his hand faded, and he opened his eyes. "He's alive."

My heart leapt.

"But not necessarily well."

My heart pounded. "What do you mean? Is he sick? Is he dying?"

Asher deposited the slip of paper in my hand, then leaned back on the bench. "Not exactly, but there's something off about his register. His aura felt dark, troubled."

I bit my lip. "That makes sense. He's been depressed since my mom died, and he's been doing a lot of drinking. Well, more than he's used to."

"That must be it. Whatever it is, it's taking its toll on his mind, his body, his spirit."

I stared at the piece of paper in my hand, then looked up piteously at Herald.

"No," Herald said, frowning. "Absolutely not. You're thinking of seeing him, aren't you?"

I barely had a chance to open my mouth when Herald cut in again.

"You're forgetting the part where you're supposed to be dead. Well and truly dead, as far as the normals are concerned. What about the Veil, Dustin?"

"Fuck the Veil," I spat.

The Lorica was so keen to keep up appearances, to ensure that the rest of Valero, no, that the rest of the human world didn't know about the arcane underground that coexisted in the same layer of reality as the regular world.

The Veil was the pact we mages held to keep regular humans – the normals – from learning about the supernatural. But the city had already been invaded by shrikes once, and its botanical gardens grown over with a hell-plant the size of a skyscraper.

How often could the Lorica send out its Mouths to erase the normals' memories, to make them forget what they saw? And what did that grand scale of destruction and fuckery matter in the end if it meant that I didn't have the chance to patch things up with my father? That was all I wanted. I'd fight to protect Valero, and I'd fight to stop Thea, but reconnecting with my dad? Didn't I deserve that one little thing?

But before I could put any of that into words, a motorcycle revved its engine, pulling up angrily, it felt like, to the sidewalk. It was the kind of noise that belonged to a machine that belonged to a man who loved nothing more than the adoration and attention of the general public.

Ugh.

"Don't look now," Herald said. "Here comes Bastion."

It was anyone's guess, really, how he could find us so easily, but Sebastion Brandt had worked at the Lorica long enough to establish a sort of clout. That meant that he had a little influence over the Eyes, enough to ask them for small favors about locating a certain extremely handsome shadow mage. As big of a douche as he was, Bastion had just enough charm to get his way. Shame that it was offset by such a terrible personality.

He leapt off his bike then ripped off his helmet, the one with the blue flames on the side, shaking his blond hair loose like he thought he was in some perfume commercial. But there was something slightly different about Bastion that day. Normally he would have taken his time to saunter, savoring the opportunity to taunt me. But this time he was walking towards me briskly. A little too briskly. And his hands were both in fists.

"Oh," Asher said. "He looks super pissed, dude."

"Really? What tipped you off?" I fingered my jacket and picked it up off the bench, ready to shadowstep in case this meant real trouble.

"I think he wants to rip your head off."

My ass had barely left the bench when Bastion grabbed me by the collar. He pulled me uncomfortably close, eyes piercing, cheeks red as he stared me down.

"The fuck were you thinking, Graves?"

I held my hands up. "Wow. Okay. Nice to see you too, Brandt."

The last time we saw each other was at a getting-to-know-you dinner hosted by Carver, one that was meant to forge slightly friendlier ties between the Boneyard and the few members of the Lorica I considered my closer friends.

Nothing about Bastion was very friendly in that moment.

"Bastion, put him down."

I knew that voice. I stood on my toes and stretched my neck as far as it could go, watching as Prudence Leung hopped out of a car and hurried towards us. Her hair sailed in the breeze as she ran, and I watched her fists for the telltale blue mantle of fire that meant she was about to punch shit and break it apart. Nothing there today, fortunately.

"What the hell is going on?" Herald said. Asher only watched, transfixed.

Bastion, as if he would ever let anyone forget, was among the Lorica's most powerful Hands. Prudence was one of them, too. He was telekinetic, able to lift and tear things apart with just the force of his mind, while Prudence could wreathe her fists and her feet in mystic flame, then use her martial arts expertise to utterly crush and break things, from bricks to bones. Both, incidentally, were also fairly skilled magic users, which only complicated matters.

"I said put him down, Bastion." Prudence stood with her hands at her hips, breathing heavily, winded from her run. "There's got to be a logical explanation for this. We're not sure that Dust did it."

"Did what?" I pulled a finger under my collar, wondering when Bastion was going to finally let go of me.

"I thought we agreed to stay out of each other's hair," he said. "You stick to your business, and we stick to ours. That includes not breaking into my family's mansion to steal heirlooms." He stabbed a finger at my chest, way too close to the scar Thea left above my heart. Bad move.

"I don't know what the fuck you're talking about." I shoved Bastion in the chest with both hands, something he clearly didn't expect – or appreciate. His face reddened even further as he stumbled away from me. And did he say mansion? "Prudence. What's he talking about? You've got your head on straight. I'm sure you can explain without acting like a complete gorilla."

Bastion seethed.

Prudence rolled her eyes. "The two of you, settle. Someone broke into Brandt Manor. They riffled around the place. It seemed like they were looking for magical objects. According to the security gargoyles and the camera footage, it was someone who looked like you."

"It didn't just look like him," Bastion growled, thrusting a finger bare inches from my face. "It was him."

I swatted his hand away. "I'm sick and fucking tired of people accusing me of being places I wasn't." I laughed, though it was totally humorless, the kind of chuckle that spills out of you from disbelief and exasperation. "And Brandt Manor? Is that some kind of joke?"

Prudence shook her head. Bastion looked like he was about to burst into flames. Herald shrugged. Asher looked between us, eyes wide.

"Wait." I said, my voice softer. "Your family has a manor?" I was curious. I mean, aren't you?

"Not the point, Graves. Now tell me why you broke in, and tell me what you wanted. No one endangers my family like that."

Bastion waved his hand across his face, palm outward, and slivers of shimmering energy trailed in the motion. Around us, the air gleamed, as if it had been turned into glass. Prudence groaned, and I followed suit.

This was Bastion's favorite thing as of late. He specialized in two things. The first was using his ability to pick up and throw things as projectiles, turning something as innocent as loose pebbles into a hail of gunfire. The second – and he was good at this part, too – was erecting invisible shields, which made him both an offensive and defensive asset to the Lorica.

The problem was that he'd also learned to create much larger shields. They were domes, in fact, that cloaked their occupants from the world outside, casting a magical glamour in a large area. Bastion had gotten quite proficient in camouflaging territory in this way, allowing arcane grudges to be settled in relative privacy by disguising the blasts of energy and brilliant fire that typically marked a mage's duel.

He wanted to fight, is what I'm saying. Bastion casting a dome was the equivalent of a frat boy pressing his face up against yours and grunting "Let's take this outside, bruh."

"Let's do this," Bastion said. Ah, close enough.

"Listen," I said. "I'm not going to fight you because I have nothing to fight about. I didn't break into your ridiculous mansion."

Bastion threw his hands out, then clenched his

fingers. The sound of wood warping and cracking broke the silence. Asher yelped as Herald tugged him off the park bench, and just in time. The bench flew apart, beams, bolts, all its component pieces bursting into splinters under Bastion's power.

Typical Bastion. Shoot first, ask questions later. No, let me be more specific. Bastion's style is to shoot something full of holes, then shoot some more. If it's still alive, maybe ask it some questions. Then whether or not it answers: shoot it dead.

"Move back," I heard Herald mutter to Asher, somewhere behind me. "Brandt's power has a functional limit to its range. We move out of the way, we'll be fine."

"Bastion, stop," Prudence shouted, her hands already emanating their signature blue flames. It was likely only a threat to get her partner to stand down, but I never thought I'd see the day the two would possibly, maybe butt heads.

Bastion cried out in frustration, then lowered his hands. The sharp, horrible pieces of broken bench fell to the ground in a crash of splinters and sawdust.

I huffed, brushing at my clothes. "So are you gonna pay for that bench, or were you going to put it back together?"

Sometimes – not often – I wish I could remember that shutting the fuck up was the best option.

Bastion socked me in the chin. It's hazy now, but I vaguely recall exclaiming "Ack" in a clipped voice, because a blinding, bone-deep pain immediately began radiating from my jaw. I clutched at my face, stumbling away, my feet tangling in bits of broken park bench. Instinctively, I was already seeking out the nearest shadow.

Prudence shoved Bastion, grabbing at his jacket, but he kept advancing.

"Bastion, will you stop?" He wouldn't, shrugging Prudence off – no small feat, considering she was basically the equal of a werewolf in a fistfight. Bastion lifted his fist and stalked straight for me.

I kind of hated that my magic really only had two settings: run, or kill. Carver could put people to sleep, disintegrate their weapons to disarm them, or, in a really tight pinch, break half the bones in their body. I wanted that kind of defensive magic, the stuff I could use to neuter someone, but not necessarily kill them dead.

But before I could react, Herald snapped his fingers. The purple mist around his hand blew away in the sudden, freezing gust of wind that sheared through Heinsite Park. The chill left as quickly as it came, but I realized that Herald wasn't just literally trying to cool things down. Bastion was grunting, struggling to pull his legs out of the huge chunks of ice encasing his feet and fusing him to the ground.

Yeah. That kind of magic. That was what I wanted.

"Get this shit off me," Bastion shouted. "Prue. Break this and let me – "

"No," Prudence said. "Frankly speaking, you're being a brat. We have no hard evidence that Dust was behind this. Give him the benefit of the doubt. It could have been a glamour. And if you're just going to lash out by beating up on him you can – "

"You're only saying that because you're dating his roommate."

A sharp chill, colder even than Herald's spell, blew through the park. Maybe the sky even darkened a little. For the first time that afternoon, I saw something cowed in Bastion's expression, like he realized he'd royally fucked up.

Prudence's voice cut like ice. "You quit this bullshit, Sebastion Brandt. Here and now. Or I report this to the Lorica."

In a tiny, meek voice, Bastion answered. "You wouldn't dare."

"You destroyed public property. You attacked another arcane person unprovoked. Do you think that being a Hand means you're above the law? Lower the field, or I swear, Bastion. I'll do it."

He gestured at his feet, helpless, struggling, throwing Herald the occasional threatening glance. Herald only smirked back.

"You wait for it to melt," Prudence said. "Sun's

out. I don't care. Give you some time to think about what you did."

I clutched my jaw, letting it unhinge, not even sure how angry I was. Maybe I was shocked. I just felt numb. I knew that Bastion and I had always butted heads, but it had never come to blows like this. Two break-ins by someone who looked like me. First that Salimah woman, and now some mansion? What the hell was going on?

The air shimmered, proof that Bastion had lowered his field. A stray dog yowled at us, surprised that five people had just blinked into existence. It turned tail, then ran off.

Herald tugged on my jacket, hauling me away from the park. Asher followed quietly.

"Yeah," Bastion said. "You better run. This isn't over."

"Sure isn't," I said. "See you, Bastion. Watch your back."

The problem with Bastion was how much he liked to hit.

My problem was that I was learning to like hitting back.

Chapter 5

I sighed as verdant green energy rushed from Asher's fingers, seeping into my skin. I could feel tendrils curling into my cells, sinking through my muscle and down into my bones. My nerves began to numb, or perhaps the pain began to vanish as his magic cleared away whatever damage Bastion had done to my jaw.

I didn't know why the Lorica looked down on necromancy and considered it so dangerous. If this was necromancy, then it was awesome as far as I was concerned.

Asher leaned back, his eyes narrowing. "Question. And stop me if it's a stupid one, but – why didn't you tell those Lorica people that it was Thea behind it?"

I rubbed at my jaw, still surprised at how

quickly Asher's treatment had taken effect. "Honestly? As much as I know that it's a possibility, we don't really know that it's her modus operandi to go around impersonating me now. I mean, to what end? I don't know that we should be causing a panic without knowing a hundred percent."

Asher rubbed his nose. "I mean, I do."

"You think so?"

"If there's any chance that it was Thea? Sure. Knowing what she's capable of, I would have spoken up."

I bit my lip and stared at the ground. "I guess it's hard to think straight when someone's clocked you in the jaw, you know? Can't lie, that probably jarred my brains around a little."

"You should give them a call, the Lorica people. Text them. Keep them updated. Can't hurt to have everyone on alert, you know?"

I honestly couldn't think why I hadn't considered to do exactly what Asher was recommending. He patted me on the shoulder, as if sensing my thoughts.

"Maybe your brains were jerked around more than you thought. It's not a problem. Just call as soon as you can."

"Right," I said, still somewhat mystified. "Right."

I reached for my phone as Asher strode out. I managed to mutter a belated "Thanks" just as he was shutting my bedroom door. My fingers moved on autopilot, typing out a message to Herald that roughly conveyed what Asher had suggested. "Should we tell them about Thea?" Send.

Don't know about you, but that's always the part I hate the most: waiting for a damn reply. I stared at my phone's screen for a minute too long, willing Herald to respond, waiting for that little checkmark under my message to turn green so I knew that he'd read it. But nothing. Ugh.

I tossed my phone onto my bed, my head craning in the direction of my shelves as I did. Man. It always happened this way. I'd be alone in my room, and I'd do everything I could to pretend that he wasn't there, but without fail my mind and my eyes would always wander to that one shelf in the corner by the standing lamp.

Once, when he was alive, that shelf was Vanitas's place of honor. His own bed, to put it in different terms. It bothered me knowing that his body still sat broken on the stone shelf, a mess of shards and twisted, tarnished bronze, just shattered garnets mingled with bent bits of green-gold metal. It haunted me knowing I couldn't do anything, that Herald and I hadn't found some way we could bring him back.

But we still talked. It's still considered a conversation when only one person does all the talking, right? Sad, I know, just a boy and his broken sword, going slowly crazy over the extended silence. Sometimes I wondered if it was easiest to pretend that Vanitas was never enchanted, that the talking had all been in my head.

"I dunno what to do, V." I folded my arms behind my head and flopped down onto my pillow. "I mean, surely Thea isn't that stupid. She wouldn't be that bold about wearing my face and going around attracting attention to herself, right? That's just ridiculous."

In the silences, my mind filled in the blanks. What would Vanitas say? Probably something about how I was a dumb idiot, and he wouldn't be wrong.

I chuckled, staring at a spot on the ceiling. "I talk about this whole doppelganger deal but I think we both know I've got something else on my mind." I reached inside my jacket pocket, feeling around for the little scroll of paper I'd cracked out of Arachne's gift.

Was it the right time? It'd been so long, and now that I had a lead — no, not just any lead, but my father's actual, new home address — something was in the way. All those concerns from months back, from when I'd just been murdered came rushing in again. How would he react? What would he say? Would he even want to talk to his son's walking corpse?

My phone vibrated, and my hand flew quickly to pick it up, but it wasn't a text from Herald. It was a phone call from — Prudence? I frowned at my phone. Knowing her, she could have put the pieces of the puzzle together on her own without any prompting from Herald whatsoever. I swiped and picked up.

Not one word had left my mouth before her voice was already crackling out of my earpiece. "You'd better not be involved in this, Graves."

"I – I'm sorry?"

"I don't know what's going on here, but this is just too creepy. I'm at my grandma's antique shop, out in Little China, and her surveillance footage shows that you were just here."

"That's impossible. I'm – " I stopped. What the hell was I supposed to say? No one outside of my roommates was supposed to know about the Boneyard. "I'm far, far away from Little China right now."

"Then get your ass here right now. We need to figure this out, and fast. Something funky is going on."

"It's Thea," I said. "It has to be. Remember how she masqueraded as someone else last time we saw her?"

The line was silent. Thea had disguised herself as the assistant to Enrietta Boules, an agriculture magnate and a dryad businesswoman hiding in plain sight in the normal world. After weeks, maybe months of impersonating the dryad's PA, Thea revealed herself and murdered her in cold blood, right in front of us.

"If that's true," Prudence said, slowly, "then this is bigger than we thought. In any case, come over. We need to talk. And you – you should really see the footage." Another pause. "I'll text you the address. Come quickly."

I shoved my phone back in my pocket and practically vaulted off my bed, reaching for the stone shelf before stopping myself. That's right. Vanitas was gone. I sighed, then rushed out of my room, down the corridor to the portal leading back into Valero.

Mama Rosa's Finest Filipino Food was completely dark, the way it was supposed to be after closing time. Mama Rosa herself had gone home. The others had to deal with the triple-padlock system she had in place to protect the establishment, but I could simply shadowstep out.

And that was exactly what I did, shifting through the ethers and emerging almost instantly on the sidewalk outside the restaurant. I bit my tongue to stop the yelp from escaping my throat when a slender white hand landed square in the middle of my chest.

"And exactly where do you think you're going?" Sterling asked.

"Somewhere. Out." I tried to push my way past, but he stood firmly in my path. I frowned. Sterling was as solid as a brick wall, and just as dense and as stubborn.

"Don't think so."

"Dude. Out of my way. You know I can just shadowstep past you, right?"

Sterling sucked at his teeth, his eyes rolling. "Like I couldn't catch you if you tried. I'm faster than you." He loomed closer, eyes glinting with feral curiosity. "Where are you going, anyway? Tell me. I'm bored."

"You're not coming."

"Am too."

I sighed. Dense, stubborn, etcetera. "Prudence called me. Whatever that Salimah lady complained about with running into someone who looked like me? Prue says the same thing. Someone tried to break into her grandma's shop tonight, over in Little China."

Sterling guffawed. "And you're just going to show up, alone? Just like that? What if it's a trap? Or what if it really was that Thea psycho in disguise?"

"It's – if it was Thea, then I'd have backup. And Prudence is still a friend. She wouldn't set a trap for me." I looked down at my hands, then back up at Sterling. "Right?"

He folded his arms slowly, his brow creasing as he did. "You going out there just because she called is the dumbest thing I've ever heard."

The blood rose to my cheeks. "Say what you want, but it's not going to stop me. Get out of my way."

To my surprise, Sterling stepped aside wordlessly. It made me stop in my tracks. I guess I was expecting a fight. He saw the look on my face, and shrugged.

"I'm not going to stop you."

"You're going to tell, aren't you?" I stabbed a finger at his chest and regretted it almost immediately. Dead bodies were freezing cold, especially in the evening Valero chill, and vampires were no exception. It was like poking a slab of ice. "You're gonna stay here and blab."

Sterling chuckled and swatted my hand aside. "I'm not that petty, Graves. Not everyone gives that much of a shit about you."

Something glimmered in my chest, bright and hopeful. "So – so you think I could be doing the right thing?"

He laughed. "It's a terrible idea. Probably the worst you've ever had." He brought his Zippo to his cigarette, and flicked. "I'll come with."

"You – I don't – "

He shoved me in the back. "Shut the fuck up and lead the way."

I stopped, squinting at him. "Why are you being so nice to me? Why are you coming along?"

He shrugged. "I'm trying this new thing where I try to be a good teammate." He grinned, fangs gleaming in the streetlight. "And if there's a fight – well, I could always eat."

Chapter 6

"There's this great xiao long bao place just down that street."

I eyed Sterling cautiously. I'd been there once for soup dumplings, with Thea, of all people. "You sure know a lot about food for a dead guy."

"We've been through this. I don't process calories." He puffed on his cigarette, then stubbed it out on the sidewalk. "And you sure need a lot of bodyguarding for someone who's supposed to be a mage."

That stung more than it should have. "Hey. I didn't ask you to come with me, so – "

"Shh. Shut your stupid mouth, we're here."

Here was the outside of a Chinese apothecary, a nondescript little shop with wood-clad windows, one of which was shattered, the asphalt lined in fragments of glass. The store shone warmly from the inside, incandescence spilling onto the dew-damp sidewalk. Little brass chimes tinkled as Prudence pushed her way through the door.

"Look at this mess," she said, lips tight with annoyance, though she must have known that I didn't have anything to do with it. If I was responsible, would I really have come back to the scene of the crime? "My grandmother's terrified."

"I'm – sorry? I really don't know what to say, except that I didn't do this."

Prudence's eyes were still hard, but she spoke kindly. "No, I know. I believe. But did you have to bring this one with you?"

"Hey," Sterling said, one finger raised. "You'd think I'd get better treatment now that you're dating my buddy, but no. It's prejudiced. You're prejudiced."

Prudence groaned. The door chime tinkled again, and this time Gil emerged. I honestly shouldn't have been surprised that he was already there.

"He's cool," Gil said, patting Prudence on the shoulder. "Hardly ever shuts up, but Sterling's cool." He nodded at me, then at the glass on the ground. "Whoever's dressing up as you did a number on Madam Chien's shop."

I peered through the store, trying to get a glimpse of Madam Chien, but nothing. I lifted my head at the lone security camera staring me in the face, then gave it my best grin.

"She's my grandmother on my father's side," Prudence said. "I love her to death and I know she's just really upset by this."

"Let's go talk to her, then." Sterling swept past our huddle, already slinking his way into the apothecary. Prudence followed hotly, like she was worried he might do something to Madam Chien. Gil only gave me a shrug.

"Come on in," he said. "I think everyone's a little shaken. Madam Chien rushed here when she found out something was wrong, then she called Prue to come over. I happened to be, um, with her at the time, so."

I smiled. "No need to explain. Glad to know you guys are getting along. No more beating each other up."

He scratched the back of his neck, grinning sheepishly. "Well, I mean, that depends on what you mean by beating – "

I smiled so hard I must have sprained my neck. "No need to explain. Honestly. Please. Stop."

"Gotcha."

Madam Chien's apothecary glowed like a lamp, lit with old light bulbs that pulsed like braziers, like little fires. It was the kind of place that permanently smelled like incense, the austere aura of an antique store combined with the comforting must and dust of an old bookshop.

It wasn't the strangest assessment. The apothecary was way more than just your standard assortment of ginseng and wolf berries, filled as it was with unusual decor, things in jars, illustrations of the human body on yellowing sheets of paper wrapped in cellophane. Still, it was warm in a way, almost welcoming. I could imagine spending the night and not minding it much.

Behind the counter, wizened and wiry, her hair a snow-white cloud, sat Madam Chien. Her pursed lips showed the impression of someone who permanently disapproved of everything, starting with me. Her eyes narrowed as I approached the counter.

"Him," she said. "He did it."

"Grandma, I'm telling you, that's not possible. Dustin's our friend." Prudence shook her head, waving me over. "I'm sorry, she's just so frightened. She's a wreck right now."

"It's okay," I said, forcing a smile.

I studied Madam Chien. Frightened wasn't quite the right word to describe her. Frankly, she looked pretty relaxed for someone whose place of business had just been broken into. She did look at least a little pissed off. She seemed just about ready to smack my head right off my shoulders.

"Come here, Dust," Prudence said. "You should see this."

Madam Chien folded her hands together as I stepped closer, her lips puckering even tighter. I couldn't be sure if her tunic was what she wore day-to-day, or if it served as her sleepwear since she'd probably woken in response to her security system going off, but it gave her the appearance of a martial artist.

Peering out of one of her sleeves was a tattoo of what I thought was an arrowhead. On closer inspection, it turned out to be the head of a dragon. She scowled and slipped her hand over it when she caught me looking. I bowed my head in what I hoped passed for an apology.

"This is why she's so suspicious. Look."

Prudence tapped at the screen of a laptop that was quite a few generations out of date, but still recent enough to run the security camera's software. It was a blur at first, the figure walking from the other side of the street, but as he came into focus, the breath caught in my throat.

The man – thing, whatever he was – looked to either side of him, then up at the security camera. I looked into my own face as it grimaced, then made a small grin.

"Holy shit," I murmured.

Sterling made a nervous chuckle. "That's messed up. Look at that, Graves. That's creepy as hell. Right, Graves? Oh crap, I'd be shitting myself."

"Make him stop," Prudence said.

In my peripheral vision I caught Gil elbowing Sterling in the stomach. I knew Sterling was just being himself – a douchebag – and trying to freak me out, but I was still too focused on the thing in front of the camera to engage.

Other-Dustin took off his jacket, wrapped his fist in it, then punched clear through the window. He disappeared off-camera, then less than a minute later, reappeared with something bundled under his arm, dashing off into the night.

"He's paying for my window," Madam Chien muttered.

"Grandma, I told you, it can't be him. Dust wouldn't need to break a window."

The old woman harrumphed and folded her arms. Prudence groaned.

"Dust, would you please just show her?"

I blinked. What, just shadowstep, like a performing monkey? "Uh, I'm not sure about this."

"It's cool. She's one of us."

I blinked again. Huh. Somehow it never occurred to me that Madam Chien could have been a mage. Did magic run in the family? Was there something about arcane blood that I didn't know? I filed them away as questions to ask Carver, or maybe Herald, later on.

I decided to go simple and quick. I picked a shadow near a medicine cabinet, one of those ornately carved ones with dozens of miniature drawers. Maintaining eye contact with Madam Chien, I sank into my own shadow on the ground, jaunted as quickly as I could through the Dark

Room, then emerged just inches from the cabinet.

My hands spread to either side of me, I waggled my fingers, a silent, half-hearted ta-da. Showing her my magic trick only reminded me that there was someone out there wearing my own damn face, the difference being that I could shadowstep, and they couldn't.

"I don't see your point," Madam Chien grumbled. "Your Uncle Stephen could teleport, until that time he was stupid and showed up in the middle of traffic."

Aha! I fucking knew it happened. Teleportation mishaps weren't just urban legends after all.

"The point is, grandma," Prudence said, through gritted teeth. "The point is, he could have just teleported in. He didn't need to break the glass."

Madam Chien barked something back in Mandarin, which set Prudence off, and the two went at it. The guys and I stared off into the corners of the apothecary for some uncomfortable seconds, caught in the crossfire of a familial spat.

But all of that just raised another question. If it was Thea impersonating me, then surely she wouldn't have resorted to something as crude as punching through a window. Well, shit.

"Fine. Fine. So it wasn't him. That doesn't help. I want my peach back."

"You'll get it back, Grandma. We just need to track whoever it was down."

"Get one of your Eyes to do it. What good is the Lorica if it can't even help us in this matter?"

I looked around the store. "Wait. That's right. Where's the Lorica? Or the cops, for that matter? You said something about a security system."

"I wanted to handle this before reporting anything to the Lorica," Prudence said. "I don't want the authorities in on this. Neither does Grandma. Her system is more of a series of wards that she put up herself," she continued, gesturing at a number of yellow paper talismans pasted around the apothecary. "The security camera is really the only nonmagical precaution we have in place."

"We," I said. "So this is a family business?"

"One hopes," Madam Chien said, eyeing Prudence meaningfully. "My son and his wife are doctors, but this one here decided her place was with the Lorica, punching and kicking things for pleasure."

"I don't do it for fun, Grandma," Prudence said icily.

"You should put those days of danger behind you, the way that I did. What's so wrong about running the store, the way I do? There is great pride in our business. When will you learn, Mei Ling?"

I raised an eyebrow. "Mei Ling?"

Prudence blushed.

"Leung Mei Ling," Gil offered. "It's her Chinese name."

It was kind of cute that he knew that about her. The two of them made an oddly sweet couple, honestly, if you didn't think too far about the possibility of magical flaming werewolf babies in their future.

"You guys," Sterling called out. "Come here."

None of us had noticed that he'd sauntered off to examine the broken window. I stepped over, spotting the glinting glass shard in his hand. On its edge was the smallest trace of blood, easy enough to miss in the dark on the damp sidewalk.

Gil slapped himself on the forehead. "I should have noticed that." He gave Prudence an apologetic glance. "I don't know how I didn't notice that."

"Because it isn't regular blood. Nothing in the conventional sense, at least. Hard to sniff out." Sterling dragged the shard lightly across his tongue. I felt like I was the only one cringing at the sight of him doing it. He smacked his lips a couple of times. "Ugh. It's bland. Lifeless." He nodded at me. "Almost reminds me of how you taste, Graves. Almost."

Every head in the apothecary turned slowly in my direction. Prudence folded her arms, a cheeky grin blooming on her face, the kind that asked: "Is there something you aren't telling us?"

"Look, he stole it from me when I was injured, okay?" I threw my hands up. "It's not like I let him chew on my neck or anything. I'm not a cow."

Madam Chien brushed me aside with a surprisingly powerful stroke of her arm as she went to examine the bloodied shard. "I don't judge," she said, an absent grin in the corners of her lips. "It's a very modern arrangement," she continued, waggling her eyebrows at Sterling, then at me.

Sterling nodded. "I know, right? So progressive."

"Please stop," I said. "There's nothing going on between – "

Madam Chien waved a hand. "So you can find my peach?"

Sterling looked to Prudence for an answer.

"A jade peach," Prudence said. "It's an heirloom artifact, passed down from our ancestors. Its enchantment is very specific – most mages won't even find a use for it. But it belongs to our family."

"And it passes to Mei Ling next," Madam Chien said. "If only she would marry."

"Grandma!"

Madam Chien's features hardened, and I braced myself for another angry Mandarin tirade, but it didn't come. "I don't care if you marry this wolf boy here. Times are changed. Did I ask you to find a Chinese boy? No. But I want to see you married before I die," she said, a patently false tremble in her voice. "And wolf boy will do. He will give you tall, strong babies." She sniffed. "Latin American-Chinese babies. Very modern."

"So progressive," Sterling cooed.

"We should track down the culprit," Gil said, his ears flaming red, his smile so fake and tight he could have ground his teeth down to powder.

"No. No." Madam Chien shook her finger for emphasis. "You stay here with me, with Prudence. You help me clean up, close shop. Blood boy and his boyfriend can track down the peach."

"I swear nothing's happening – "

"Come on, sweetheart," Sterling trilled, slinging an arm over my shoulder. "Let's go kill your doppelganger."

Chapter 7

Sterling held the bloodied glass shard in front of him like a totem. It glinted in the streetlight as we moved, a crimson diamond in the palm of his hand. Every so often he would hold it up to his face, sniffing quietly, or flicking his tongue out to sample the blood. Then he'd point down a street or an alleyway, following the shard like it was a dowsing rod.

I was pretty sure he had no idea what the fuck he was doing. Either that, or there was a vampire bloodhound quality to him that I'd never known about. I left the possibility open. There was still so much that I needed to learn about the arcane and the supernatural, after all.

He wasn't afraid of silver, for example, which was why he wore so much damn jewelry, like the wannabe rockstar that he was. He was a fan of garlic, especially when Mama Rosa made up a batch of beef salpicao, which was essentially beef drowned in butter, Worcester sauce, and garlic.

Sunlight was devastatingly dangerous for him, though, something I'd seen him suffer twice. That second time totally didn't involve a harebrained gambit that also resulted in the destruction of an artifact belonging to the Japanese sun goddess Amaterasu. Based on our playful and often wildly offensive banter, I knew that both fire and a stake in the heart could kill him, too.

Sterling held the shard up again, looking through it like a lens, or maybe he was studying the blood, gleaning whatever there was to glean from the bare traces of it that remained.

"This way," he said. And like a moron I followed along without a word.

Despite never hearing about his blood-sensing skills, I knew that Sterling was a seasoned hunter. He was a beast of prey, at heart, something which fundamentally allowed him and Gil to get along in spite of their differences in attitude. It was weird knowing that the gentlest member of the Boneyard, at least before Asher came along, was our resident werewolf.

But again, what linked the two of them was the fact that they were both truly, innately killers, apex predators at the top of their respective food chains. In a way I was almost relieved that Gil hadn't come along, because when we found

Other-Dustin, between the three of us, there was a good chance he was going to end up dead. And I had questions.

If it truly was Thea, then we would have a fight on our hands. But again it was so unlikely. Smashing shit up just wasn't her style. If this impostor was someone – or, let's be realistic here, something else – then Sterling would want to play his wicked games.

It was bizarre how territorial he could get about the Boneyard and its constituents, but I was getting the impression that vampires were clannish like that. Even Carver said so. It was strange to think of Sterling as less of a monster knowing that part of him valued his tribe so much, how absolutely fucking feral he got each time we encountered Bastion, knowing he was such a threat. And if tonight meant that we would be in danger –

"We're close," he muttered.

I looked around, chewing my lip as I understood exactly where "close" was. We'd wound up on the edge of the Gridiron somehow, Valero's industrial district, no small feat considering we'd gone the entire way on foot.

"Are you sure about this?" I gathered my jacket around myself, shuddering. I didn't think to wear anything thicker, not imagining that we would spend so much time away from the Boneyard, but it was well past midnight by then.

"You've got your magic, I've got mine."

I squinted. "All you've done is lick a piece of glass all night and we're barely even close. I'm ninety percent sure that you're just making shit up so we mmff – "

Having Sterling's hand clamped over my mouth was an odd and frankly terrifying feeling. The best way to describe it was having a dry and weirdly smooth frozen lamb chop pressed over my face. I struggled, my protestations muffled, but he gripped harder. He lifted a finger, pushed it against his lips, then pointed across the street.

Someone approximately my height and build had just ambled across the sidewalk. It was too far to make out any real features, but I could see the same ill-fitting jacket that I'd seen on the apothecary's security footage, the same strange gait. Other-Dustin kept walking, slipping into the darkness of a warehouse. I kept my eyes glued to his back. At least we knew that the thing couldn't shadowstep.

"That's our man," Sterling said.

Grunting, I slapped his hand away, wiping at my face with the sleeve of my jacket. Who knew where his fingers had been? But more importantly, I had a thumping sensation of dread in my chest. I wanted this horse shit with all these cases of mistaken identity to end.

I didn't need vampires accosting me in dark alleys when I was just going out for a burger, and I still owed Bastion a punch in the face. Yet I knew somewhere inside me that confronting

Other-Dustin was going to result in some kind of catastrophic mess.

I frowned at Sterling as he dipped the shard in his mouth again. "Will you please stop licking that damn thing?" I half-wished he'd cut himself on it, just so he would stop.

He ignored me, his eyes turned curiously up to the sky. "The blood tastes wrong. Almost — artificial. Soulless."

"So stop licking it then."

"Never."

Sterling dashed across the street, his feet soundless against the asphalt. I'd long accepted that I would probably never get used to how fast he could move, just a bolt of leather and silver streaking through the darkness.

Call it cheating, but I felt more secure when the two of us were walking abreast of each other, so I shadowstepped to keep pace, emerging in the darkness of the same warehouse Other-Dustin had entered. Sterling stood there, his face raised to the shadowy walls of the structure.

"Abandoned," he whispered. "You'd think the owners would make more of an effort. Renovate, sell it on, rent it, something."

"What do you know about business and real estate?" I hissed. "Plus, shut up. We're trying to be sneaky about this."

"I know plenty. Also, no, you shut up." He raised his nose in the air and took a slow, deliberate breath. "He's still in there. Flank him.

You creep in through the left entrance. I'll take the right."

The left entrance being the ramshackle remains of one of those sliding shutter doors, clinging for dear life onto the battered, chipped wall. I should point out that we weren't working in total darkness. It was shadier there since we were technically in an alleyway between buildings, but there were still streetlights. The moon was out, and for whatever you could see over the glare of a city's lights, so were the stars.

Yet as I crept all I could think of was how Sterling had once told me that we worked best in darkness, him, myself, and Gil. They used their superior senses, and maybe through some affinity with the shadows, I had better than average vision in gloomy situations myself.

And in that darkness I saw him. Traces of movement came from among the splintered crates and pallets sitting like capsized ships in the shadows. Other-Dustin, this thing that was wearing my face, was rocking on his feet, his hands cupped close to his lips, so close that his cheeks glowed with the same jade-green of the artifact nestled in his palms.

I began the slow, arduous duck walk I knew I needed to use to creep up on him. En route I picked up a loose plank, careful to dislodge it soundlessly from its brethren, weighing it in my hand. One sound smack and I could probably knock the thing out with a Sneaky Dustin Special.

But as I approached, I became more and more consumed with the notion that all this stealth, and the pincer attack Sterling suggested, weren't all that necessary.

The creature wasn't very bright. Madam Chien's apothecary was only three blocks away. Other-Dustin was clearly in a rush to spend time with the peach, a fact only supported by how he started petting it like a mouse in the palm of his hand. And when I thought things couldn't get weirder, Other-Dustin brought the peach to his face, nuzzling it against his cheek. I gripped the board tighter, splinters pushing into my palm. This was going to be easy.

But then his eyes flew open.

Have you ever seen one of those horror movies where the hero's just brushing his teeth, or flossing, maybe, minding his own business, when out of nowhere his reflection's mouth curves into a sinister, demonic smile?

That's what this was. That's what happened. My heart was punching against the inside of my body, thumping at the sight of my own fucking face grinning at me with too-wide lips and far too much unfriendly intent. And in the jade light of the peach it was easy to see that his eyes were black. Jet black.

Mine were supposed to be blue. His eyes darted at me, like he always knew I was there. He wasn't supposed to see me coming. He wasn't supposed to hear me.

He wasn't supposed to move so fast.

Chapter 8

In only two quick bounds the creature had closed the distance between us, his free arm winding up to strike. No time to panic, or for the yelp to move past my lips. I sank into the shadows, stepping into the Dark Room, the air displacing over my head as the creature missed its blow.

My lungs fought for breath as I shuffled through the tunnel of the Dark Room, board still in hand. It was hard enough to breathe there, and I didn't need the uncertainty of what I was fighting to complicate things further. But tell me, how would you react to finding a near-perfect copy of yourself that wanted to kill you?

I clenched my fingers tighter over the plank as I reemerged in reality, crouched in a section of the warehouse at least a couple dozen feet away from where I had left Other-Dustin. Sweat slid in trickles down my nape as I surveyed the darkness for the beacon of green light that should have given him away, but he was missing.

Did he escape? Unlikely. The look on his face was thick with malice. No. Not his. It. This thing wasn't me, wasn't a man. I refused to accept that it was human. It knew who I was, and it drew pleasure from knowing that I was so disconcerted by its existence.

Something scraped against the ground. The thing was behind me, its leer grotesque, its teeth a sickly green in the light of the peach still clutched in its hand. I spun on my heel and swung the board with all my might. Other-Dustin raised its other hand to intercept the board, making a fist – and punched clear through the wood.

Fuck.

Broken splinters of wood clattered to the ground. Other-Dustin shook its fist back into an open hand, knuckles specked with blood, then aimed another blow at my face. I dodged, scampering backwards into the darkness, my eyes glued to the creature even as it trundled and bore down on me.

No way. There was no chance in hell that it could have been Thea. She was prone to speeches, the big damn villain that she was, and to shows of bravado. Brilliant spears of light, spells meant to destroy. But this thing was coming at me with everything its body could give, every swipe and surge of its extremities another attempt to kill and to maim.

Other-Dustin rushed me again, reaching for my collar, tugging at me with an infernal strength. I wasn't that strong. Shit, no human should be that strong. My eyes darted around the darkness of the warehouse, scoping out Sterling's position.

Where the fuck was he? I wasn't going to out him. If there was one tactic we stuck to at the Boneyard, it was never letting the enemy know how many of us were present. It made them overconfident, and ultimately, easier to overwhelm and subdue. But if Sterling didn't come soon –

Stall. That was the best I could do. If shit got real, I could slip away into the Dark Room. That would work, wouldn't it? It only had me by my collar. Fuck, why didn't I test this with someone from the Boneyard?

I already knew the answer, though: they liked me well enough, but not enough to risk getting dragged to an alternate dimension full of shadows and blades that would rip them to pieces, with or without my command.

"What do you want?" I croaked, the gathered fabric of my shirt and jacket cutting into my throat.

"What do you want?" the thing said, in my voice, with my mouth. But its eyes, God, its eyes were all wrong.

"Who are you?"

The thing's grin dropped, and it tilted its head. Its hair fell away from its eyes, gleaming and black.

"Who are you?" it said, the words cold, and coarse. Could it only repeat things? It brought its face closer to mine. Other-Dustin was panting, as if the contact was exhilarating, as if excited by the imminent promise of violence. Its breath misted on my cheek. It was colder than the night air. My skin prickled.

Fuck. Fuck. "What are you?"

The thing grimaced. Evidently, that was the wrong thing to say.

"What are you?" it parroted, its voice high and short as it grabbed my clothing tighter, beginning to shake me. "What are you?" it demanded, its voice – my voice – shrill and breaking, spittle forming at the corner of its mouth. "What are you?"

I didn't know. On some level I understood that the creature could only repeat what I said, but it cut me to hear those same horrible words from my own mouth. What was I? Hecate said so: I was an abomination. A beautiful monster. And what was it that monsters did?

I lifted my hand to the thing's shirt, to the tattered assortment of clothes it had put on its body, searching for a spot of material that wasn't drenched in its ice-cold sweat. It followed my hands with wild, black eyes. The fire I lit with my hands reflected in those eyes, turning them into coals, black and orange and smoldering.

Other-Dustin shrieked, beating at its clothes, doing a horrible dance as it stamped and flailed, one hand thrashing at the flames licking at its body, the other still cradling the Leung family's artifact.

It flailed and screamed, body ablaze, slamming itself against the walls to smother the fire. For whatever reason its desperate bid to survive was working. Maybe it was the sweat soaked through its clothing that helped, or maybe it was some bizarre, inhuman instinct to live on.

It came at me again, burnt skin exposed through incinerated patches of its shirt, no more dead, but a whole lot angrier. I thought I had time to shadowstep, but it lunged, leaping for my throat. The two of us crashed to the ground, my back slamming painfully across the concrete. It straddled me, thighs locking around my chest and my ribcage. The thing clasped one too-strong hand around my throat, then started to press.

"What are you?" it croaked, pushing down on my neck so hard that my head ground into the cement. I groaned in pain, except that there wasn't much air left to groan with. Wheezing, choking, I grabbed at Other-Dustin's wrist, but nothing. It was far too strong.

Nothing for it, then. I had to shadowstep, whether or not it meant taking the thing with me.

I willed myself to melt into the earth, to pass through my own shadow into the Dark Room, and my heart thumped ever faster when I realized I couldn't.

I simply fucking couldn't. The lining between that reality and this one held fast, the first time since I'd awakened to my talent that the membrane between worlds was impenetrable. I couldn't take Other-Dustin with me. I couldn't shadowstep, and with cold, stark dread, I realized what was worse – I was going to die.

Then a crack, and a faint exhalation of air. Other-Dustin grunted, the gleam in its eyes fading, the strength in its grip fading even faster as it wavered, then collapsed backward. I gasped, sucking at the world for air, relishing its sweetness as it came rushing back into my lungs. I clutched at my throat, breathing deeply, deeper still. I was alive. At least one of us was.

Sterling stood over the both of us, dusting his hands off, already reaching into his pocket for a cigarette. I stared down at Other-Dustin's corpse, at how its neck was positioned at a completely unnatural angle.

"You killed it. You snapped its neck."

Sterling took a long draw of his cigarette, then exhaled a stream that vanished into the high ceiling of the warehouse. "Thank you, Captain Obvious."

Death wasn't the result I had wanted. I had no intention of killing the thing. It might have known something. But even as I watched its limp body, studied the grim lifelessness of its black eyes, I knew that this creature wasn't anything normal, not some human mage in disguise, not a magical thing hiding under a glamour. Then what was it? Had an entity sent it to cause trouble for me via impersonation? Worse, had the entity sent it to kill me?

"You should have acted more decisively," Sterling huffed. "That could have gone so much more badly for you."

"But we could have captured it. We could have questioned it."

"You could have died, you idiot."

I bit my lip, my eyes focused on the ground. "Yeah. Okay."

Sterling sighed, an irritated, long-suffering sound. "Thank you for saving my life, Sterling. Thank you for disposing of the thing that was trying to kill me. You're so strong, and brave, and handsome."

I rubbed at the soreness on my neck, already sure it was developing into a bruise. "Thanks," I muttered.

He grunted, sifting through his pockets. I frowned when I realized what he had retrieved from inside his jacket.

"A syringe?" And a pair of phials.

"I might get hungry."

"Sterling. That's disgusting, even for you."

He rolled his eyes again. "It was a joke. We

might be able to use this thing's blood. Just trust me on this for once." He kicked the corpse, as if to test whether it was truly dead, then bent low to begin his extraction. "I'm sure it won't mind."

I turned away, suddenly squeamish at the sight of Sterling very nearly desecrating what very well could have been my corpse. I should have had the balls to do it myself – to kill it – but I hesitated. Maybe I was afraid. But I didn't need the flames, nor did I need to shadowstep to escape.

All I needed to do was hone my connection to the Dark Room, to open just enough of a gap between it and our reality, and I could call a blade of gleaming shadow to kill it in one strike. But I didn't. Fuck it, I couldn't. How do you kill something that has its own face? Hell. How do you kill something that wears your face?

Sterling rose from the floor, pocketing his effects, then nudging the corpse with his boot once more. It almost felt like he was getting a kick out of it because it looked so much like me.

Then the corpse moved.

Sterling sprang towards me, hauling me by the back of my jacket with his horrific vampire strength until we were safely away from Other-Dustin's twitching, convulsing remains.

But it wasn't coming back to life. Smoke rose from the thing's body, hissing and churning, and I bit back my revulsion when I realized that the corpse was melting, disassembling into its fluid components right before our eyes.

The smell of burning meat filled my nostrils, and I fought the urge to retch. The last of its organic matter bubbled and burbled on the cement, and the smoke cleared. All that was left of the creature was a puddle of gore.

"Holy shit," I muttered.

Sterling tugged on my collar, pulling my face uncomfortably close to his. He thrust one hand out at the puddle. "This won't be the last of this, Graves, and the next time you run into one of those things, you need to be ready to end the fight quickly."

"I set it on fire," I mumbled. "What more do you want from me? What more do you want me to do?"

"Show that you're not afraid of some magic trick. Show that you can handle your clones." Sterling stabbed a finger at Other-Dustin's remains, then released me roughly, his eyes twin points of steel, his voice like the edge of a blade. "It's simple. The next time this happens? Kill yourself."

Chapter 9

God but I couldn't get the stench of burning meat out of my nose. The walk back to Madam Chien's apothecary had done its work of replenishing the air in my lungs with something almost fresher, but it stuck to me still, lingering like a terrible memory. Barbecued flesh, simmering fat and skin, hair scorched to cinders. Worst of all was not knowing whether it was human.

And Sterling was no help at all. He'd taken up the task of describing Other-Dustin's death to Prudence and the others with a little too much excitement. Madam Chien's face screwed into something very much like a dried plum as Sterling went on, gesticulating wildly and placing emphasis on how he very much enjoyed killing my mirror image.

Even Gil was cringing at the retelling, as if I needed further evidence to signify how utterly fucked up this all was. I'd watched someone with my own face die right before me. It made me wonder if I would look like that when I died, with my mouth half open, drool at the corner of my lips, my eyes unfocused and glazed. Those terrible black eyes.

"A doppelganger," Madam Chien said. "That does not bode well for you, shadow boy." She pushed her fists into her waist, surveying her shop. The broken glass had been cleaned up, at least.

Prudence shrugged. "It's already dead. Isn't that what they say? You're fine if the doppelganger dies."

I knew she was trying to be supportive, but it hardly helped, knowing what Sterling had said about the possibility of there being more of those things out there. Surely the same creature couldn't have stolen the Heartstopper, then broken into Bastion's place, and then Madam Chien's, all in such a small span of time.

"Could be fae," Gil offered, sweeping at an already clean floor with a broom. "Which is even worse. A changeling? Cripes, it could be anything. It just needed a glamour."

"The fae would have left something behind. A token, a corpse, something to tie their bodies to their realm." Sterling shook his head. "I'm telling you, this thing practically dissolved."

"Carver," I breathed, finding my voice at last. "If anyone has an answer, Carver does."

Gil deposited his broom in a closet by the counter. "You two head back to the Boneyard and ask him, then."

"The Boneyard?" Prudence quirked an eyebrow.

"Long story. But best option there is. You guys go talk to Carver. Prue and I will stay here with Madam Chien until morning, or at least until someone shows up to fix the window."

Madam Chien patted the back of his hand, her eyes brightening as she grinned. "Such a good boy. You'll make a good husband. Stay here. I'll make tea."

Gil blushed crimson. I grinned, but the smile dropped clear off my face when Prudence lifted her finger and rushed me.

"Behave," she said.

I raised my hands, backing away. "Hey. I didn't say nothing."

Her finger thrust past my head. "No. About that."

I followed where her finger was pointing. The grimace came naturally to my face. I wasn't expecting Bastion to be standing on the sidewalk outside the apothecary. Sterling followed my line of sight, and I could tell that his posture tightened.

The Boneyard and our "friends" at the Lorica might have broken bread together once, but it was clear that Sterling was still a bit sore about that one time Bastion dropped a car on him.

"Hey," I told Prudence, clenching my fist. "He threw the first punch, okay? I didn't even get to hit him back."

"Just — he looks sorry, okay? At least I think he is. Look at the dumb idiot."

I did. Bastion's shoulders were rounded, his hands stuffed in the pockets of his leather jacket. Even his hair, normally styled to looked mussed and effortless, seemed limp. I squinted at him, and grumbled. This was by design.

The fucker needed something from me. I could say whatever I wanted about disliking Bastion Brandt, but I couldn't call him stupid. He had his own brand of cunning, and I hated to admit that it was working — at least at raising my hackles.

I gave Madam Chien and the others a curt nod, then pushed my way through the front door. The door chimes tinkled, then again as Sterling followed cautiously, sticking weirdly close to my back. Bastion's lips were pursed. He looked up at me, back down at the sidewalk, then scuffed one of his shoes against the ground. The asshole. I knew that trick, too.

"All right, Brandt. Spit it out. You want something, just say it."

"I'm sorry."

I'll be real, that caught me off guard.

"I mean it. I'm genuinely sorry. I shouldn't have lashed out at you like I did."

"Lashed out is an interesting way to put it," I said, rubbing my jaw. Asher really did a great job. I thought there'd be bruising at the very least, but I felt fine. "So. You need something. You wouldn't have shown up here past midnight if you didn't."

Bastion clenched his jaw. Ah, I knew it. His eyes flitted from Sterling, then back to me. "Okay. But not here. We need to talk. Ride with me." He thumbed over his shoulder.

I'm not sure how I hadn't noticed the black luxury sedan parked right behind him. I was just going to ask where his motorcycle was when an older man stepped out of the driver's seat, then opened the rear door, his head bowed slightly.

"Huh," Sterling said. "Fancy."

"He's coming with," I said, patting Sterling on the shoulder.

Bastion frowned. "Really? Is that necessary?"

Sterling hissed. Vampire instincts, I guess. Old habits die hard.

"Can't hurt, can it? I'd feel safer. Shit's going down in Valero, man. You've obviously heard about Prudence's grandma, or you wouldn't have known where to find us."

"Fine. Just – fine. Hurry and get in."

Sterling slipped into the car first, and I followed, ending up sandwiched between him and Bastion. The first thing I noticed were the leather seats. Firm, but somehow luxuriously buttery. The second was the minibar. The third, when the driver climbed back in, was the fact that he was wearing gloves.

"Either you're planning to murder me somewhere nice and private, or this is the beginning of a very interesting party."

"Neither." Bastion leaned forward, and in the calmest, kindest voice I'd ever heard, spoke again. "Remington? Home, please."

The driver bowed his head of white hair, muttering something that sounded very much like "Yes, sir."

I eyed Bastion incredulously. "This is like the snazziest rideshare I've ever been in. Does the Lorica pay for this?"

Bastion chuckled. "Please. I don't need the Lorica paying for my shit."

Realization dawned. I should have figured it out sooner. This was a chauffeured car. My very first impression of Bastion being a brat raised in a mansion by nannies was on the nose after all. His family was super rich. Which meant –

"We're heading to Brandt Manor, aren't we?" I felt silly just saying that out loud.

Bastion nodded. Sterling snorted. "Seriously? Brandt Manor? That's ridiculous. You're ridiculous."

"If you say so," Bastion said, sinking back into the seats, sifting through the bar. "Cocktail, anyone?' He gave Sterling a passably sympathetic look. "I'm sorry, we don't have plasma, though. Can I offer you a Bloody Mary?"

"Bite me," Sterling grumbled.

"So Brandt Manor is totally real, right?" It sounded so farfetched. What kind of family had a named estate? Rich people, that's who. Crazy, rich people.

"Absolutely. It's where I've lived all my life." He transferred some ice into a glass, then tipped in a can of diet soda. "You'll have to forgive the mess though. Mother's having some work done on the helipad."

Chapter 10

"How do I not know this about you?" I waved around myself, my sneakers looking so utterly pedestrian against the polished cobbles of Brandt Manor's driveway. "How come none of us have ever heard of your family? Jesus, is that a tennis court?"

Bastion followed my finger, then shook his head. "Badminton, actually. We don't talk about it much, that's why."

I blinked. "You're the most self-absorbed, conceited human being I've ever met. That doesn't make sense."

He shrugged. "We keep to ourselves. We don't display our wealth." He cleared his throat, perhaps aware of how insincere he sounded with his family's hedge maze standing just a few dozen feet away. "People have heard of the Brandts, but it's not because of the money. Besides, sometimes you have to look beyond yourself, Graves. Sometimes, it's about protecting family."

He turned away, beckoning us to the mansion that must have had at least twelve bedrooms – and that was just in the front. "Family." He'd said the word with a curious mix of gravity, and awe, and spite.

It made me want to rear up and poke him in the chest. Who the hell was he to say that I didn't know anything about family? But I just grumbled to myself, following as he took the first of several steps leading up to the front door.

We'd hardly reached the top landing when one of the double doors creaked open, which was kind of a shame. I was very curious about the brass knockers set into each door, the ones shaped like the heads of lions. Maybe it's childish to admit that I kind of wanted to use the knockers myself, but really, when else was I going to get a chance?

"Master Brandt," the man said, his head bowing slightly. A butler? Had to be. His eyes swept over Sterling, then me, and he smiled in that polite kind of way that said you were welcome, but only if you didn't put your feet up on the ottomans.

Bastion nodded. "Silas."

We followed closely as Silas ushered us through the front door. I only just caught a glimpse of how he was also wearing white gloves before he slunk off and disappeared into a side entrance. I couldn't tell you which of the doors he vanished into, if I'm honest, because there were a lot of them. Far too many.

I've infiltrated mansions before. You know that. We've been through those places together, the ones owned by wealthy reality TV stars who'd just come into money, or by manic California party people who snorted their inheritance and burned their wealth on huge Roman orgies. None of those compared to the heart-wrenching opulence of Brandt Manor.

I gaped openly at its marble floors, its rich wood-paneled walls, at ceilings that were far too high to dust yet still looked spotless, at the chandeliers dripping with crystal. I followed the curve of the grand, sweeping staircase that connected the already massive first floor to a second level that, beyond my comprehension, looked even more lavishly decorated.

Brandt Manor was a castle, and I was a nose-picking peasant who'd happened to wander in by accident. Even through the soles of my sneakers I could sense the chill emanating from the marble, the cool, refined temperature of old money.

On top of everything bizarre I'd already encountered in the arcane underground, it had to be something so mundane that put the cherry on top. But that's inaccurate. I don't know that you could look at Brandt Manor, at the family sigil of a lion that welcomed us at the front gate that was now prominently displayed on a frigging heraldic shield over the fireplace, at anything in this picture of ridiculous grandeur and think that it was anything approaching normal.

But a woman appeared at the top of the staircase, and as she descended, the word "mundane" and all of its sibling synonyms vanished. She didn't descend, actually. Float might have been more correct. And not in a metaphoric sense, either, because this woman, clad in a flimsy dressing robe thrown over a silk shift, was literally floating down the stairs, her body suspended a few inches in the air.

If you had told me that slow, seductive jazz played in the background as I gawked at her, I would have believed you. She was a deeply attractive older woman, the kind of lady who might accurately be described as a mother I'd like to – um, follow on social media.

In one hand she held a glass of something clear and brown. She watched me as she sipped, as if sizing me up, her eyes maintaining their searing contact over the rim of her glass. They reminded me of Bastion's, flecked with the same brutal, unshakeable confidence. Her hair was the same blond. As Sterling and I were to find out, that wasn't where their similarities ended.

"Mother," Bastion said, his tone flat, but soft enough to be respectful, though not enough to be affectionate. It's strange how much you can glean from a single word, if you pay attention.

"Sebastion," the woman said. There was fondness there, to be sure, but it was hidden behind a thin sheet of ice. "You've brought guests."

Mrs. Brandt said the word in a way that suggested we were welcome, as long as we didn't leave with our pockets jangling with their expensive silverware.

"You didn't have to make such a grand entrance," Bastion said.

Mrs. Brandt held her hand to her chest, feigning surprise. "Oh, was it grand?" She turned to me, then Sterling, the same mocking lilt in her voice. "Was I being grand, gentlemen?"

I shook my head, meaning to be polite. Sterling grinned, and drawled. "Oh, yeah. Grand's one way of putting it."

The corner of Mrs. Brandt's lips lifted in a grin. That was a wink she gave Sterling. It must have been. I fought hard not to look Bastion right in the face to see how he was reacting, but out of the corner of my eye I could tell that his skin was going red.

The foyer was silent again. The single, perfect sphere of ice in Mrs. Brandt's drink clinked as she took another sip. She held the glass at waist level as she floated lower, her feet finally touching the ground. The ice clinked again.

"You haven't introduced me to your friends, Bastion."

He scoffed. "I'd hardly call them friends. But whatever. This is my mother, Luella Brandt." He nodded at Sterling. "This one's Sterling. That's all you need to know about him."

Sterling grinned again, making no effort to hide his fangs. Luella bowed her head and returned a smile of her own.

"And this one's Dustin. We used to work together at the Lorica."

"Pleasure to meet you, Mrs. Brandt."

"Please, call me Luella." Her eyes widened. "And 'used to,' is that what I heard?"

"Yes, ma'am. I was a Hound back when I was still working for them. I have, um, a different employer now."

Luella threw her head back and guffawed. "You see, Sebastion? There's life after the Lorica after all." She gripped her glass in both hands as she sashayed towards me, leaning in conspiratorially. "I tell him that he wastes his potential there, but he never listens," she whispered, loud enough for everyone in the foyer to hear. Her breath smelled like expensive whiskey, and a hint of cinnamon.

"Mother, please don't start."

"Start what?" Luella held her hand against her chest again. The splay of her delicate fingers against the curve of her breastbone made her almost birdlike, and the sentiment of her words innocent. But I could see the hawkish intent in her eyes. "Start another perfectly reasonable discussion about why you're wasting your life for the Lorica's sake? That last incident with that Morgana woman was unacceptable, Sebastion, and if you think for one minute – "

Luella stopped mid-breath, the talon of her finger pointed directly at Bastion's chest, and she said nothing more. A lot had been at risk in our most recent brush with the mad sorceress named Thea Morgana, once my mentor, once my murderer. My life was in danger, as was Bastion's, though none of us came closer to mortal peril than Asher. Luella's lashes fluttered, and she seemed to remember herself. Sterling stood perfectly still. I cleared my throat as quietly as I could.

"Not in front of guests, mother," Bastion said. His voice came out softly, his shoulders hunched. I'd never seen him sad before. I wrenched my gaze away.

"I – apologize, gentlemen. I can get quite carried away when the subject of Sebastion's father comes up."

I bit my tongue as hard as I could to avoid stating the obvious. No one had brought him up. But Luella answered anyway.

"He was killed in action working as a Hand for the Lorica. We lost him years ago, but every day I remember him still."

I didn't know that about Bastion. I realized there was a lot I didn't know about him, least of all that we'd both lost a parent.

Luella turned her head, her eyes lingering on the portrait over the mantle. Painted there was a younger version of herself, holding the hand of a preteen Bastion. Behind them, standing proud, was a man I imagined Bastion would look like in thirty years. He was striking, imperious, his hair flecked with gray. Power radiated from his eyes. How a painting can do that, I couldn't tell you, but I caught Sterling staring as well.

"He was a great man," Luella murmured. "Strong. Handsome." She curled her hand into a fist, the ball of ice in her glass clinking as she gritted her teeth. "Vital, and powerful. One of the strongest the Lorica has ever known. He could have been a Scion."

Scions were the highest ranking of mages in the Lorica, at least that I knew of. I'd only ever met one, Odessa, a Scion who specialized in creating mystical shields. Looking back, Thea might have qualified as a Scion as well. I never bothered to ask what her rank was. It was unimportant then, back when I believed she was a friend and mentor to me.

Bastion's lips were still pressed together, his eyes cautiously avoiding mine and Sterling's, his gaze glued to the floor, his ears burning crimson. Luella reached out and made a motion with her hand that looked as if she was stroking the air. She stood several feet away, but Bastion's hair lifted up and out of his face, as if swept by an invisible hand. Ah. Maybe magical talent was genetic after all.

"I only want what's best for you, Sebastion. And in my opinion, that does not involve a life led with the Lorica. You have no use for employment, nor for money. All your needs are paid for. Why do you put yourself in so much danger for the same faceless organization that killed your father?"

Bastion bit his lip, his hand in a loose fist. "Because they still do good, mother. They can help, even in things like this break-in." His eyes flashed to me, then to a far corner of the mansion's atrium.

It was a familiar sight. Moonlight streamed in through what was once a beautiful bay window. It was broken now, shards of glass strewn across the marble floor, over the plush seat in the window's sill, scattered across the books set in the same alcove. The wind blew gently outside, but even with the window broken, the fine, gauzy drapes stayed perfectly still.

"We cast a barrier as a precaution," Luella said, as if in answer to my unspoken question. She lifted her glass to her lips, about to take a sip, when she seemed to remember something else. "And before you ask why we don't sustain a magical wall at all times, you try maintaining a household staff of twenty and having to lower the damn field every time a chauffeur drives in or the gardener pops out."

Did she say twenty?

"So you've had a break-in as well," Sterling said, sweeping off to inspect the broken window. He made no effort to hide that he was sniffing at the air. He was looking for the same traces of blood. I caught him patting at his jacket, as if to check that the phial of corruption he drew from Other-Dustin's corpse was still there. "What were they after?"

Luella huffed. "Pick something. I wouldn't have minded if they made off with something less valuable, but the thing was headed directly for the family repository downstairs, like it knew exactly where to go." She raised her glass at me and winked. "It had your face, you know."

A chill trickled down my spine. "Then how did you know it wasn't me?"

"Because I took one of its hands." She drained the last of her whiskey, then dismissed it with a wave. The glass hovered away and clinked as it settled onto the mantlepiece. "You may have seen how my son operates. Our talents are similar." She clasped her hands together, skin flushed with alcohol, and beamed. "But he's far more gifted. My precious baby."

Bastion scratched the back of his head, his neck flushing. "Mother. Please."

"So powerful. So handsome." All hints of pride vanished from Luella's face, and her cheeks became etched with vitriol. "And yet he squanders all his time and energy with the Lorica."

"The hand," Sterling piped up. I liked to think that he did it specifically to save Bastion from another tongue-lashing. I had no way to prove that, of course. Maybe he just wanted to get on with it. "Where did it go?"

"Oh," Luella said. "That's the best part. I caught the thing as it was escaping. Its hand fell into the bushes outside the window. Wouldn't you know, it dissolved into the ground. Just a pile of sludge, and then nothing. The gardener says it might have salted the earth."

Sterling and I exchanged glances. As if we didn't already know that Other-Dustin and the thing that came to Brandt Manor were related.

"That's why I needed to apologize," Bastion mumbled in my general direction. "I blamed you for something you didn't do."

"Wouldn't be the first time you were a jerk to me," I said. Luella made something halfway between a chuckle and a snort. "But okay. Let's just figure out what we can do about this."

"Agreed," Luella said. "Bastion wasn't home when the burglar came. I intercepted him – it – as the thing was leaving the family vault. It might have broken into the manor, but breaking into our repository takes much more effort, that's for certain. I chased it out through the same window it used to enter, and that's when I severed its hand."

Sterling craned his head, surveying the atrium slowly, his gaze finally resting on a bookcase.

"There. Is that where it entered?"

"Why, yes." Luella gave him another of her sticky grins. Bastion said nothing, but I felt the room warm just the slightest. "If you gentlemen will follow."

I tried to hide my surprise when Luella headed directly for the bookcase in question, then kept walking, disappearing as her body moved among the books. It was a glamour. Sterling shrugged, then followed. I leaned in, curious about stepping through the illusory wall myself, when Bastion's hand landed on my shoulder.

"Just so we're clear," he said, his voice uncharacteristically soft, his eyes still on the ground. "We're all good, right, you and me?"

I rubbed my jaw where, not hours before, his knuckles had connected with my face. Lest we've forgotten: my precious, beautiful face. "You totally sucker-punched me, though."

He frowned. "You don't seriously expect me to let you hit me back, right?"

I gave him a slow, deliberate wink, and said nothing. I stepped through the bookcase, melting into the glamour. In my pocket, my hand clenched into a fist. I absolutely wanted to get him back for that – I just wasn't going to say how, or when. Bastion shuffled after me uncertainly, making small, confused noises.

This was going to be fun.

Chapter 11

Imagine a wine cellar, except that there are no casks in it, no bottles lining endless shelves. Imagine a basement, with walls carved out of smooth stone, like a tunnel in a pyramid, or the storm drain leading out of some abandoned research facility. Imagine a crypt.

It was cold in the repository, and dark, so much that even I had difficulty seeing clearly. The time I'd spent in the Dark Room had honed my senses just enough to let me see better in gloom, but the chamber that the Brandts kept under their sumptuous mansion was like the pit itself. Soundless, except for our footsteps, except for our breath. And cold. Exceedingly cold.

Luella muttered a string of words I couldn't make out, the rush of them tumbling from her lips with the low whisper and rattling crackle of twigs catching on fire. A globe of flame appeared about a foot away from her head, suspended there like lamplight.

I blinked to adjust, and when Sterling flinched away, I planted my hands on his back in what I hoped was a reassuring manner. He looked at me over his shoulders, his eyes all jittery, but he kept walking when I nudged him. I couldn't blame the guy.

Sterling and fire had a bit of bad history, between him being incinerated by a beam of sunlight, and being nearly obliterated when a miniature sun appeared just feet above him. Also there was that one time when a cigarette exploded in his face.

I hate to admit that I was involved in at least two — okay, all of those situations, but that was part of what made Sterling and I closer, morbid as it sounds. He drank a bit of my blood, so I set him on fire a little. You don't know that you're really friends until you've fought a little, am I right? Eye for an eye and all that.

The tunnel didn't go on as long as I expected, and we ended up at a stone wall that carried a relief of the Brandt family's leonine crest. Dark, pinpoint stains dotted its surface, which when I realized that the other Other-Dustin didn't have a chance of breaking into the family vault even if it slammed its head repeatedly against the wall. The entrance was magically sealed, and there was only one way to gain access.

"You do it, Sebastion," Luella said. "Mommy's been hitting the sauce a little too hard tonight. If I prick myself I may just spray blood all over the place."

I didn't know if alcohol actually did make blood thinner, or pump faster, but the sheer mention of letting seemed to have an effect on Sterling. He made a small sound in the back of his throat, then threw me an uncertain, sidewards glance.

"Fucking behave," I muttered, softly enough that the others wouldn't hear.

Bastion tutted, shaking his head at his mother as he brought two of his fingers together. Before they could even meet, just inches apart, one of them bloomed with a perfect bead of dark blood, as if pricked with an invisible knife. Sterling shuddered, then pushed his fist against his mouth, biting at his knuckles.

"Sterling. Honestly. Get a grip."

"I'm trying," he said, his voice thick with desire.

Bastion incanted softly to himself, then pressed his bloodied finger into the relief, his blood joining the other tiny splotches scattered across the stone. The walls around us rumbled, like great, stone gears were turning inside of them, the hidden mechanism groaning like some ancient beast. The Brandt crest rotated some degrees, then with some effort, slid slowly apart, stone grinding against stone, a thin cloud of dust lingering in the breach where the seal once stood.

The Brandts stepped through the gap. Sterling stayed still, even after I pushed on his shoulders.

"Dude. Come on."

He didn't budge, just watching mother and son longingly as Bastion stuck his finger in his mouth and nursed his pinprick wound.

"Oh my God, Sterling, you're the worst. Stay here until you get your shit together."

"Yeah," he murmured, scratching the back of his neck and smoothing down the creases in his jeans. "Yeah, I'll be fine, be right with you."

And sure, contextually I guess I understood where he was coming from. Vampires liked being able to sample blood from unusual sources, whether that meant mythical creatures, supernatural beings, or mages. Bastion's blood must have been even more tempting, considering the immense arcane power that flowed through his veins.

Just how much power the Brandts held, however, I didn't truly grasp until I stepped into their family vault.

Lights were slowly coming on high up in the ceiling, gradually revealing the interior of a room filled wall-to-wall with display cases, each containing a different artifact, and each artifact, no doubt, filled with deep stores of supernatural potential. A cursory calculation told me that there must have been at least thirty cases in the vault, many of them holding pieces of jewelry, dusty grimoires, even one or two weapons.

This was like a section of the Gallery, the massive library found in the Lorica headquarters where their archivists stored all their confiscated artifacts and enchanted relics. The Brandts had their own miniature Gallery in the basement of their manor, and it was small testament to both their wealth and their power.

The whistle that escaped my lips tumbled around the room. Both Luella and Bastion turned to me at the sound of it, giving me satisfied and somewhat smug glances. And for once, I wasn't mad about it. I didn't need to be told what each item in the vault could do to guess that it was a formidable collection. It was an arcane artillery stockpile that would have been brutally dangerous in the wrong hands.

"So this is why you were so protective," I said, nodding at Mrs. Brandt. "It's why you went so far as to take someone's hand."

"Holy shit," Sterling said, having finally calmed himself and joined us in the repository.

"Indeed," Luella said. "My actions might have been extreme, considering the thing had a snowball's chance in hell of breaking its way into the family vault. But it's the principle of it, you know?"

"We are nothing without our pride," Bastion said.

"Nothing without our pride," Luella echoed, pointing at the Brandt family crest embedded in one of the walls, at the lion's head that watched us stoically. "My husband would have done so much worse. He would have severed the creature's legs. Maybe taken its heart."

"Sounds like my kind of guy," Sterling said absently, peering into the display case of a gem that throbbed with an internal light, pulsing rhythmically, its azure glow rippling like water across the glass.

"He was irreplaceable," Luella sighed. "As irreplaceable as the treasures we keep here. Heirlooms, nearly all of them, crafted by our ancestors, if not won as trophies in battle. By rights no one should know about this chamber. It's a family secret, and I trust the two of you will be prudent enough to keep it that way."

I nodded. Sterling, nose now pressed up against a different display case, put up two fingers. "Scout's honor."

"We have a theory about these doppelgangers of yours, Dustin." Bastion gestured around the room. "The family vault is warded. Think of it like a recording studio. Sound doesn't come out, the way that arcane energy doesn't leak out of this place. Even the Eyes couldn't find us here. There's only one thing in this entire room that we can't mask, and that's because of its, well, unique properties."

He beckoned us to the far end of the room, to

a display case that looked like all the others. Inside was a nondescript blade, short, like a dagger, and without a hilt.

"This is the Null Dagger," Luella said. "Shaped like a throwing knife, which is really the only effective way to use the thing. And the reason our spells cannot cloak it is because of its own unique enchantment. It dampens magic in a field around itself. A very small field, yes, but one strong enough that it cancels nearly all known magic."

Sterling scratched his chin, making it look like he was in deep thought as he fingered his non-beard. "That hardly seems useful."

"Well, normally, yes," Luella said. "But if the right person knew how to wield this thing, they could disable a mage simply by poking them with it. Like I said, the dampening field is small, but stab someone with it, and make sure it hangs in there? Then even a wizard is only as good as a helpless child."

I frowned as I stared at the thing, then frowned harder when I raised a hand over its display case. Something definitely felt off. It was as if the air was filled with static, and my hand was moving through a cloud of fuzzy, invisible fibers. My eyes met with Bastion's, and something from months ago came flooding back to me. It seemed to come back to him, too.

"That reminds me," he said, cocking his head. "Whatever happened to that pocketknife I lent you? The one you used to draw blood for Hecate's summoning?"

"Oh. Yeah. Carver destroyed it, the same night I almost killed him with one of Herald's lightning bottles."

Bastion tutted, then shook his head. "You owe me a knife, Graves. That was a good one, too. About the same weight as the Null Dagger."

I narrowed my eyes. "I always wondered about that. You can do miracles with your talent, yet you carried that knife around in your pocket. What gives?"

Luella watched us with interest, and Sterling wandered off again, with marked disinterest. The peaks of Bastion's cheeks reddened.

"I guess it was practice, for when I can find a use for the Null Dagger. You know, lay it down somewhere, levitate it, then throw it at someone? If a mage doesn't see it coming, that's a quick, easy way to disable them."

Luella patted the back of his hand. "It's very sweet that you're trying to find some use for this wasted trinket." She looked at me, shaking her head. "We only keep it because his father won it in a duel. The point is, as strange as the dagger's properties are, it maintains a magical energy signature that someone can still read, in spite of the wards we've placed here."

I blinked at her, finally connecting the dots. "So you're suggesting that my doppelganger was attracted to its signal? That's why it came here?"

"That's the theory," Bastion said. "Look, one of

them went after Prudence's grandma. Her shop is loaded with magic. I don't think these things are picky at all. They smell something in the air, they just go for it."

Like bloodhounds. Even Diaz's artifact, the one Connor and Salimah shook me down for. The Heartstopper? That thing had a very, very specific and debatably useful function that no one would risk the ire of an entire gang of vampires just to steal. It didn't make sense until now. These doppelgangers were like magpies, drawn inexorably to arcane objects. The question was why?

A scrabbling from the wall behind us jolted me out of my thoughts. I looked to the Brandts, wondering if we'd triggered yet another secret passage in this already bizarre mystery mansion.

"She knows we're here," Luella said, her chest heaving with dismay.

"Mother," Bastion hissed, his eyes darting between myself and Sterling. "She doesn't know anything and you're well aware of that. And do we really need to discuss this here? Now?"

"They already know about the vault, Sebastion. I don't see what harm it would bring to introduce them."

"But — "

Luella ignored him as she headed for the side of the room farthest from the entrance. There was another relief of the family crest sculpted into the wall, but this one didn't have the same series of rusted blotches over its surface. Luella passed her hand over the relief, her finger pressing into an area on the lion's forehead. Something clicked, and the noise started up again, though this time the whirring and grinding wasn't quite as loud, as if the button was driving a smaller mechanism.

From behind us, Sterling muttered a curse. I bit my tongue to hold everything back when I saw what was hidden behind the second passage. It was a small room, only slightly larger than a broom closet. Its corners were lit by magical fires, the kind that gave off no heat. In the center was a cushioned pedestal. On top of it was a bizarre, horrifying sculpture of a woman, naked, formed into a strange, almost conical shape.

It was all wrong. Its limbs were fused to its body in places they logically couldn't, knees locked together, arms trapped against its torso with excess flaps of skin. And where its head might belong was a jumble of features, like an abstract painting rendered in three dimensions. The mouth was close to where the sculpture's forehead should have been placed. Two depressions that were meant to represent its eyes were placed on either side of its head, each set of eyelids without lashes, fused shut.

The eyelids flew open.

I staggered away in terror. The eyes on either side of the thing's head flickered, rolling madly, staring at everything and nothing. The sculpture shuddered, rocking in place, the cushion underneath it twisting and shuffling against the stone, and the scrabbling noise started anew.

"Gentlemen," Luella said. "I'd like you to meet my mother."

Chapter 12

I thought that coming to the Vault was going to be an exercise in awe, of witnessing the literal foundation of the Brandt family's power. I did not expect to go from bewildered wonder to abject horror in the span of so many seconds.

The woman on the plinth was alive, very much so, but she might have been better off dead. Her bulbous gray eyes rolled about in sheer terror, searching far beyond the room for something only she could see.

Imagine, for a moment, a woman made out of wax, or a candle in the shape of a human being. Now leave that figure out in the sun. Set it on a warm pavement.

Set fire to its hair.

"This is Agatha Black," Luella said. "Perhaps

one of the most powerful witches to ever walk this earth. She was my mother, and grandmother to Sebastion. A strong woman, brimming with destructive force, a sorceress with a brilliant mind." Luella's breath caught in her throat. "But even the best among us make mistakes."

This had to have been one hell of a mistake. What could cause someone to be warped as grotesquely as Agatha was? This was a husk of a person, no longer human. The thing on the plinth lurched and jerked, twitching away from threats we couldn't perceive.

Bastion made sure to catch my eye, his arms folded across his chest. For once he didn't seem like the impetuous, arrogant boy I'd always made him out to be. For once he looked like a man, albeit one tarnished by his past and his loss.

"I told you, once, that this is what happens to those who draw the attention of the Eldest. Grandmother was at the peak of her power, one of the strongest the Lorica had ever recorded. But she wanted more, much more than the entities could give her. Gods, demons, creatures of myth, none of them could have done something this cruel." Bastion shook his head, watching his grandmother with something that looked like anger, then something that looked like pity. "Only the Eldest."

I remember that night. It was just before we first contacted Hecate, in a dark alley, when we were waiting for Prudence to show up with the reagents we needed for the communion. This was what Bastion meant. Anyone who toyed with the Eldest didn't truly know what was coming to them. This was the consequence of attracting their sightless, uncaring eyes: cursed to live endlessly, blind yet all-seeing, screaming with a mouth that has no voice, in agony, undying.

"It would be more merciful to kill her," Sterling muttered. I went still as a rock. The silence was tense, and brutal, until Luella spoke again.

"You say that as if we haven't tried."

"It's the nature of the Eldest," Bastion said, his voice dropping in volume each time he uttered their name. "This was her curse, to be twisted into this form forever. And we know that she's screaming. You can't hear her, but all the time, she's screaming."

I couldn't bear to look, to see that he was telling the truth, to see the way her lips wavered and stretched taut as her mouth issued its voiceless scream. Gods knew how long she'd been screaming.

"We tried the Null Dagger," Luella said, watching her mother with pity. "That was why Sebastion liked to practice with his knife. Theoretically, we thought that damping the magic surrounding her curse would create an opening long enough for the knife to pierce both the enchantment and her heart." She shook her head. "But it didn't work. Worthless."

So that's what the pocketknife was for. I avoided Bastion's eyes carefully, and with nowhere else to look – not Agatha's suffering, nor Luella's mourning – I turned my eyes to the ground.

"Mother," Bastion said. "We should go. It isn't good for you to stay too long. You know how you get."

"It's all right, Sebastion." Her voice was hoarser. "I'll be quite all right. You go on ahead. I'll stay. Just a bit longer."

I snuck a glimpse of Luella's face then, catching the reddening around the rim of her eyes. She smiled at me tightly, then turned to Bastion again.

"I'll only be a few minutes. Make sure Silas has a fresh drink waiting for me when I come upstairs." She gazed at Agatha, then sniffled quietly. "Come to think of it, tell him to leave the bottle."

Bastion led us wordlessly out of Agatha's chamber, then in silence through the tunnel heading back into the manor. When we finally emerged in the house's foyer, he cleared his throat, then addressed me in an oddly formal way.

"So now you've been to the vault, and you've met grandmother. This has to be proof to you that I was wrong about the break-in. You have my help if you need it to stop whatever the hell is plaguing Valero. But as for Agatha? I'd rather no one else find out."

He angled his head at Sterling, waiting for a response.

"I mean this in the kindest way I can," Sterling said. "I could care less. No one will ever know."

Bastion looked at me next, his eyes as imploring as I'd ever seen them.

"Your secret's safe with me."

And that's why I felt like human garbage when, the next morning, we found ourselves back at the Boneyard, Sterling still in his bedroom avoiding the sun, and me swelling with guilt as I recounted the evening to Carver.

I don't know. I had to tell someone. He needed to know what we were up against, about both the doppelgangers that had popped up like poisonous mushrooms throughout the city, and about the thing that used to be Agatha Black.

"It feels," Carver said, "as if we draw closer and closer to the Eldest with every passing day. I won't pretend and say that things will get better or easier, Dustin. The Eldest have slept for a very, very long time, but considering recent events – and considering Thea's actions – I fear that they've set their sights on the earth once more."

We were at his desk, the one that sat in the middle of a vast, empty room within the even vaster emptiness of the Boneyard. The darkness around us, the thin space, all of it only pressed me into something smaller, less significant. A speck of dirt in the cosmos.

"If they do finally decide to step into our plane, could we even hope to fight them?" I pushed the fist of one hand into my palm, twisting it there, uncertain, and maybe slightly afraid. "Could we hope to stop them?"

Carver wore a tired smile. "There is no stopping the Eldest. We can stem the tide of their horrors. We can erect spiritual dams that will hold them, keep them at bay. We can put up walls. But everything erodes in time." He pushed his finger into the space between his brows, massaging it, shaking his head solemnly. "I think it's time I told you, Dustin. It saddens me to confess that I've been holding something back about my identity."

I didn't know if my mind could handle more surprises. I gripped the edges of my chair tight, and kept perfectly still as I waited for Carver to speak again.

"Once, a long time ago, I served the very things that we are now trying to keep away from our reality." Carver sighed, his body seeming to grow so small and so old as the air left him. "Once, a long time ago – I was a priest of the Eldest."

Chapter 13

I chuckled, somehow managing to keep the unease out of my voice.

"Aww, come on, Carver," I said, half-laughing. "You remember how to joke, right? You can't have been post-human for that long. This is the part where you throw in the punchline."

He hadn't moved a muscle. Carver only kept staring at me, his eyes unbearable and searing, cat-like and as flaringly amber as the jewels on his fingers, as those set around his stone desk.

"There's a reason I've selected this name for myself," he said, his voice flat, and remarkably bereft of humor.

I watched. I waited. He wanted me to ask exactly what lingered on my mind.

"You told me once that you were a lich," I said,

my tongue stinging at the mention of the word. It's what he was, a sorcerer who had done the unspeakable to extend his life far beyond its natural limits. That, and this new confession about his alias swirled in the back of my mind. I was sure I wasn't going to like the answer. "What – what did you do?"

Carver pinched the bridge of his nose, as if this was the first that he'd experienced any real discomfort in a long time. The way he was winding up, it also felt like this was the first he'd speak of this in ages.

"I took lives. I placed innocents upon altars, then I carved out their hearts. I keep this name as both a reminder of my crimes, and as penance."

The dread building in my body was transitioning into horror. My eyes began flitting around his office, searching for shadows I could vanish into. Just – just in case. Just to be safe.

When I opened my mouth to speak, I realized how very dry it was. "Did you do it for the Eldest?" I croaked.

"At first. Ritual magic changes very little even when it is done for things that are not of this earth. But later I did it to extend my life, because I wanted to fight back. I wanted to repent, to make my existence worth something."

He set his hand flat in front of him, palm up, then motioned in the air, as if lifting the lid off of a box that only he could see. He motioned again, like he was grasping something from out of the ethers. I gasped when I saw it. A verdigris knife, made of old, tarnished bronze, with dark garnets set into its hilt. Like Vanitas.

Like the dagger that Thea had used to kill me.

I leapt out of my seat, every muscle in my body straining to catapult me towards the one shadow I spotted by the side of Carver's desk. He gritted his teeth, spat out a single word, then flicked his wrist. Pale amber fire snaked from his fingertips, wreathing around my hands, then my ankles, then tightening, forcing me back in my chair. I opened my mouth to scream just as more of Carver's pale fire wrapped across my lips, sealing my voice in my throat.

My heart slammed against my chest in a horrible, frantic tattoo. Carver and I sat frozen there together, me out of a lack of choice, him still with one hand around the previously concealed dagger, and the other outstretched, every finger linked to the pulsing flame that restrained me.

"If you promise not to scream," he said, "I will unbind your mouth."

I glanced at my feet. There was a shadow right there. I could have melted right into it instead of leaping off the chair, and so I decided to escape through it then. But try as I could the connection to the Dark Room wouldn't hold. Carver's restraints weren't only binding my body. They had blocked my magic too, nullified it.

What choice did I have? I nodded, slowly, the

sweat trickling from my brow to the tip of my nose. He waved his hand again. Cool air rushed over my lips as his fire receded.

"I have many questions."

"Of course. But you must know that shadowstepping away from me was completely unnecessary."

"The way that you should know that restraining me with your magic was unnecessary."

Carver cocked a single eyebrow. "But was it? You were planning to run away as soon as you saw the dagger."

"Touché," I grumbled.

Carver whispered, then the flames shackling me crept back to his fingers, fading into nothing. I rubbed my wrists, scowling.

"Oh, don't be such a baby."

"They were on too tight," I said.

"I didn't want you overreacting."

I held my hands up, my eyes barely staying in my head. "News flash. I did not know any of this about you. And in case you haven't heard," I continued, thrusting a finger at the dagger in his hand, "it was one of those things that killed me."

Carver lowered the dagger, cradling it in both hands, looking, to my surprise, a little sheepish. "I admit, perhaps revealing it in the moment was too flashy."

I leaned back in my chair, feeling slightly more secure, at least for the moment. "In case you didn't know, I stayed with you specifically because I thought you weren't going to cut my heart out."

"I apologize." Carver's desk scraped, metal against stone, as he set the dagger down. Its tip was pointed away from me, as if to signify that he meant me no harm.

I stared at the dagger with macabre wonder, knowing fully well that it was a sibling of the one Thea used against me. So there were more of these things. I tapped my finger next to it.

"How many?"

Carver lowered his gaze. "How many? Do you mean the daggers?"

"Don't dodge the question. How many have you killed?"

Carver's shoulders slumped. I'd never, ever seen his confidence flag. So many firsts today. He didn't lift his head, staring directly at the dagger, but he did wave one hand.

"Show yourselves," he whispered.

I've seen some crazy shit in my time in the arcane underground. I've met gods, fought alongside a vampire and a werewolf, and stolen fire from the very sun itself. But none of that — fucking none of that could compare to the sight of the fallen dead.

Scores of them, standing around us, crowded around Carver's desk, occupying every last inch of his office, of the great stone platform that seemed to be suspended in space. If they breathed, I would have felt the air at my neck.

Men and women, children, creatures stood on two legs that I couldn't recognize, every last one of them staring off into space, each of them a pale, wavering image of how they looked in life. None were rotting, or emaciated. All were unmarked, apart from the gaping holes in their chests.

I looked around myself, my fingers digging into the armrests of my chair as if clinging for dear life. Even those bodies that stood next to me gazed on into the distance, in the same direction that Carver's desk faced.

Carver clutched at his hair, wrinkled and mussed, like I'd never seen him before. He looked weary, crumpled, changed. He stared at the dagger, not daring to look up.

"Heaven help you, Carver," I muttered.

He looked at me, eyes gleaming with a different quality now. In a voice groaning with remorse, Carver spoke. "It's far too late for that."

I looked around again, at the grating silence and stillness of the dead. "Are these their souls?"

Carver shook his head. "Only their images. I remember every life I took. Most I killed to honor the Eldest, when once I worshipped them. Many of these shades were ritual sacrifices. Many were children." His shoulders sagged lower as he said it. "The others I slew to prolong my own life. Criminals. Rapists, among them, and many murderers." He huffed bitterly, like he would only permit half of a sardonic chuckle to escape his lips. "But I wonder if that justifies any of it."

Penance. Remorse. And this finally explained why Carver was so intent on only ever disabling or subduing humans. It was how he'd behaved against the cult of the Viridian Dawn, using numerous sleep spells or magically breaking their bones instead of slaying them outright. As much disdain as he showed for the wrong kind of human, he was still staunchly on mankind's side after all.

"Do Sterling and Gil know about this?"

"They have no reason to. And I would thank you to keep this between us. They were drawn to me and my protection for other reasons. You came to me for the Eldest. You had to find out some day."

He rested his forehead in his palm, then waved his free hand. With a great sigh, as of a hundred voices exhaling, the images of the dead stuttered, then vanished into nothingness.

"Then the hideout itself – God, the very name it was given. That's why you didn't argue with Asher and Sterling."

Something that could have been a smile forced itself onto Carver's lips. "The Boneyard is a more appropriate name than they could have imagined. As for why my domicile is designed the way it is – "

I looked around us again, and I finally understood. This must have been a memory of his temple, wherever it was he came from. Every waking image of the Boneyard was a reminder. And to be so very literally haunted by the shades of those he killed, hell, even the name he took for himself? Carver's lichdom was aimed squarely at his own atonement.

"And this dagger was what I used to cut their hearts out. But you already knew that."

"Why are they so similar? This blade looks just like the one Thea used on me. It also looks like –"

"Vanitas. Your sword. Yes. And there's a simple explanation for their appearance. It's their common origin. All of them are implements of the Eldest, and of their servitors."

I sat stock-still. I don't know why I even thought to be surprised by the revelation. I'd always noted the similarities between Thea's sacrificial blade and Vanitas. I suppose I just never wanted to admit it. But then it hit me.

"There must be a reason that Vanitas attuned with me. When I went out to retrieve him for the Lorica, even Herald said that they had no records of the sword being sentient."

"That's because these tools only truly respond to those who are tied to the Eldest. And what Thea did when she stabbed you, that wasn't a lie. She implanted something within your heart, something that links you to these artifacts."

"So that's what I am now? One of their servants?"

Carver shook his head. "No. But it does mean that you are now something other than human. I struggle to explain it. This is unprecedented. I take it that this is no longer news to you, but all that I've studied suggests that you are now a hybrid."

Just like Amaterasu said, when she mentioned that I was tied to the Eldest. Just like how Hecate described me. "An abomination."

"Well, not in those terms, not quite. Though your spellcasting abilities do leave something to be desired. Quite abominable."

"Be serious."

Carver sighed. "An unfortunate joke, I admit. I apologize. The best you can do now is to listen to yourself, to control the urges within you. I sense that things have changed."

So he knew. When I killed Thea – or when I thought I did – I'd felt nothing but satisfaction. The realization of how much I enjoyed murdering her definitely fazed me. I was developing an appetite for violence. I had to wonder if it had something to do with what she planted in my heart. It only made me angrier.

"I think I need him back, Carver. I know it makes no sense, but having Vanitas around made me less violent. Less likely to kill things."

It was the objectivity of it, the knowledge that something or someone else was doing the damage instead of me. I wouldn't have to be the one snuffing out lives. In a dusty corner of my mind, I knew I could hear Hecate laughing.

"You're above that now, surely." Carver raised his nose and frowned. "You can rely on your abilities. They offer more than enough firepower for your purposes. And it pains me to admit it, but you aren't the stupidest person I know. That counts for something."

"But this isn't about arming myself. I can hone now. I can make blades out of the Dark Room like you taught me. I can make fire. This isn't about weapons. This is about bringing my friend back."

He regarded me sternly, sitting so still that I thought it was the end of our conversation. Then he sighed.

"Herald told you himself. Do not keep your hopes up. I do not know what sort of enchantment allowed the blade to keep a personality, but there is no guarantee that it will return when the sword is reforged. If it even can be reforged."

I gripped my seat harder, my chin somehow lifting even higher, like my body was trying to grow taller than Carver just to make its point.

"I have to try," I said.

"Very well. I will research a list of entities you may consider approaching for help. Though I remind you that it isn't often the best thing to owe so many favors to these beings."

"I know that," I said, managing not to stammer. "Of course I know that."

There was the distant recollection of what Arachne would ask of me if I ever beseeched her for more help in the future. And there was, of course, the slight matter of Amaterasu hypothetically being pissed at me for breaking her mirror. Carver stared at me so fixedly that I just knew he could read all that in my mind.

"Very well. As long as you know the consequences. Surely there must be a handful of entities you can consult." He waved his hand across his desk, the verdigris dagger disappearing where his fingers passed over it, vanishing back into nothingness.

"Last question," I said, my mind still processing the space where the dagger sat only seconds ago. "Are there more of these tools? These weapons?"

"I would presume," Carver said. "Though I confess that your sword is unique. I'd never seen one of its kind before. Perhaps there are others. It would do well for us to keep all that we can find."

I drummed my fingers on his table. "For your collection, I assume?"

Carver looked at me sideways. "Not at all. For our arsenal. When it comes down to it, these objects may be the best weapons we have against the Eldest and their agents." He stroked his beard, his gaze going distant. "Imagine if they sent their avatars."

The very mention of the word sent tremors crawling through my skin. Avatars were representatives of earth's entities and gods, possessing only fractions of their power. Both Hecate and Dionysus had sent their avatars to deliver messages to me in the past. I hadn't considered it, but I should have realized that the Eldest could possibly send their own avatars to do their insane bidding.

"You mean – the Eldest can bring out their own avatars? What, to herald their coming?"

"It's not something to worry about, Dustin. If you run into an avatar of the Eldest, it's already far, far too late. The mere sight of some of them would drive you utterly insane." Carver adjusted his tie, stood erect, then smiled congenially, as if his last words hadn't just filled my entire body with freezing dread, as if this entire conversation hadn't irreparably blown my mind. "Shall we break for lunch?"

Chapter 14

Mama Rosa had prepared one of her signature dishes for lunch – sinigang, a sour Filipino stew filled with vegetables, flavored with tamarind, and starring some kind of meat, anything from fish to chicken or pork. Today's sinigang featured succulent prawns, which was perfect. Sweet, crisp seafood went well with the tangy soup.

Gil, who I'd learned normally only ate raw meat when he needed to speed up his recovery process, partook of the sinigang, along with a hefty serving of rice. Carver poured boiling cupfuls down his throat, relishing how we weren't in public, where he would have to pretend to be a little more human by acknowledging mundane concerns such as the temperature of liquids. Asher relished every spoonful, his face screwing up each time he sipped.

"This is incredible. Better than my mom's."

I noticed out of the corner of my eye that Mama Rosa was reacting to what he'd said. Parts of her face, I realized, were attempting to rearrange themselves into something resembling a smile. I swear I could hear the stone of her face cracking in the attempt. It was terrifying. Asher smiled back.

We were having lunch inside of the Boneyard, at the makeshift kitchen that Carver had generously prepared for us humans. Sterling had no need for sustenance, but vampires could eat for enjoyment, and the absence of sunlight in the domicile meant that he could join us for lunch. He was mostly quiet, and honestly, quite friendly by his standards. Lunch was nice, really, even pleasant.

But nobody would deny that there was a sort of tension in the air, the awful knowing that we were just waiting for the other shoe to drop. There had been three doppelganger attacks so close together already, and that was discounting the ones we didn't know about.

It was possible that the Lorica was receiving reports on them, too, which meant that it was only a matter of time until they came down on my ass. I chewed, fresh prawn turning into rubber in my mouth, and raised my head as I swallowed, resigned to once again being marked as a fugitive by the Lorica. That was when I spotted the glimmer in the corner of the kitchen cabinets.

This had happened once before, and I knew better about what to anticipate. The sparkle came from a little blue gem that was moving, primarily because the spider in which it was embedded was also moving, sliding down a thread of silk that it was forming into a particularly complicated web.

It was one of Arachne's secret-spiders, probably come to report its findings. If this was going to go as it went the last time, it meant that the spider was going to weave the arcane equivalent of a flatscreen TV. I thought it best to warn the others.

"Guys," I said, pointing up at the ceiling.

Asher knitted his eyebrows. "The hell is that?"

The telltale amber glow coming from the end of our table told me that Carver was preparing a spell. Even worse was Mama Rosa rushing to one of the cabinets in the kitchen, rummaging quickly, then raising her arm triumphantly when she found what she was looking for: a can of bug spray.

"No no no," I cried out. Why the hell was everyone in the Boneyard so damn bloodthirsty, even Rosa? "It's a friend. It's one of Arachne's spiders. She must have information for us about the doppelgangers."

Carver stared at me momentarily, but he lowered his hand and nodded. Mama Rosa didn't move, but she held the bug spray close to her chest, wielding it like a sacred weapon. Asher shoved another spoonful of rice in his mouth, then slurped more of his soup.

The spider completed its web and settled into the center. Light radiated from its back, spreading across the web until it created the same flickering screen Arachne had once used to communicate with me in my bedroom.

"How is this happening?" Carver asked, more out of interest than indignation. It was a fair question. The Boneyard was supposed to be magically warded, after all. It was the main reason we'd never been found or raided by the Lorica.

The silhouette of Arachne's face blurred, then finally came into focus on the web-screen. "One wonders indeed. But Arachne has her ways, and my offspring have theirs. No place or person in this known world can hide its secrets from us."

"But of course," Carver said, his voice more amiable. "Welcome to our home, Arachne."

"And I thank you for your welcome, sorcerer." She angled her head, peering out of her screen, then grinned. "Ah, so many more sweetlings here today. It is good to see you again, Dustin Graves. And Asher Mayhew, too."

Asher paused from decimating his food long enough to lift a hand. "Sup."

"I won't tarry," Arachne said. "I bring word of what I've learned of the meat sacks that have dared to assume my precious sweetling's form. It appears that they are attracted to magical items, no matter how small or insignificant. Like magpies, they are, looking for treasures, for anything pretty and shiny."

"Yeah," Gil said. "We kind of figured that out."

"Ah, excellent. But have you discovered that they all come from the same source?"

"I think that should be obvious," Sterling said, in a snooty enough tone that I thought I had reason to worry about Arachne's reaction. But she only tilted her head and grinned. "The same pattern of attack, the same creature, clearly they all come from the same place."

"That much is transparent, blood-cursed. But that is not what I meant. What I wonder is whether you've realized that these creatures are created from the same stock."

I blinked. Somewhere along my spine, something cold and uncomfortable began to build. "Created? Sorry. I would have thought that this was a race of shapeshifters, or copycats wearing some really good glamours. Something like that."

"Yes," Carver said, rubbing his chin. "The phial of blood Sterling returned to me corroborates what Arachne is suggesting. These creatures are not from a different species. Their source is human in nature." He glanced at me, studying my face, but said nothing more.

Sterling's chair scraped against the stone floor as he twisted in his seat, uncharacteristically excited. "Wait a minute. Come to think of it, that thing's blood tasted kind of – familiar. Almost – wait." The chill building down my back crept further up my spine as Sterling's eyes swiveled very, very slowly in my direction.

Everyone turned to stare at me. The room went still, and dead silent, disturbed only by the flicker and sizzle of Arachne's magical screen.

"What? Why's everybody looking at – oh. Oh no."

"My sweetling," Arachne said. "These corrupted abominations are grown from the seed of your very blood."

I started to chuckle. "Haha. Real funny. Ha. Right? Guys?" No one was joining in. "Uh, guys?"

"What Arachne says points to a very real possibility," Carver said slowly. "This isn't the first I've heard of this. But to produce so many at such a rapid pace?"

Sterling clucked his tongue. Gil helpfully avoided my gaze. Mama Rosa made the sign of the cross, muttering something I couldn't understand. And Asher kept slurping.

"I leave you to discuss this among yourselves. It is a busy time for Arachne. So many places to be, people to eat."

"I, uh. Thank you, Arachne," I said.

"Think nothing of it, sweetling. At least until the next time we meet. Remember. From this point forth, Dustin Graves will always pay the fullest price."

She giggled to herself, vanishing from the screen as if she had stepped away from an arcane webcam. Then the web disintegrated, collapsing into a tangle of dust and loose silk. The secret-spider glimmered again as it climbed into a corner cabinet, then disappeared.

"Wow," Gil said. "Handy trick she's got there."

Carver nodded. "Arachne is a powerful ally. How she's able to penetrate our domicile is anyone's guess, but Dustin should be thankful for her aid."

Mama Rosa swatted at me with a rolled-up newspaper.

"Ow, geez, hey." Where did she even get that?

"No pets. Was that your pet? No pets, especially insects."

"Well technically that was an arachnid, and – hey, ouch, quit it."

"Don't care. I don't like pets. Mr. Carver doesn't like pets. Please."

"Technically that is correct. But there's no need to be upset, Mama Rosa. Dustin speaks the truth. That was simply an entity delivering a message."

"It's homunculi, isn't it?" Sterling cut in, with what I thought was an unnecessary amount of enthusiasm. "Everything she said totally points to homunculi."

"I'm afraid you're correct," Carver said. "It appears that the doppelgangers were taken from the same source. These are not creatures that have existed for ages. It is not a race of changelings or a huddle of mages with access to glamours. What we have here is an infestation of homunculi."

I cleared my throat. "You guys keep throwing that word around like it's common knowledge. What is a homunculi?"

Carver folded his hands together, setting them down in front of him on the kitchen table. I was in for a lengthy lecture. "Homunculi is the pluralized version of the term. The word you are looking for is homunculus. It's the name given to a creation made from a union of sorcerous and alchemical talent, one that results in a servant that, while capable of independent thought, is totally loyal to its master."

"And the main ingredient," Sterling said, "is usually blood."

Carver nodded. "That is correct. Though it isn't unusual to hear of alchemical recipes where the base is generated from human feces, or even semen. Normally homunculi are very small, the way you might see imps or other minor demons, but whoever is generating these clones of yours has found some method of making them human in size."

"Small?" Mama Rosa glowered, then crossed herself again. "Dios mio. I have heard of these things. We have them in the Philippines. They belong to people with bad magic. We call them tiyanak."

Asher blinked, then set his down spoon for the first time. "Hey, I've actually heard of those. Mom used to scare me with those stories when I was a kid. You mean to say she was right?"

"Of course," Rosa bellowed. "Mothers are always right. It is terrible how they make them. You take an aborted fetus, then you put it in a jar. And you give it a drop of blood every night. And when a whole month has passed – "

Mama Rosa shuddered. It was a strange sight, because I'd never thought her capable of being frightened of anything. And that, naturally, gave me more cause for concern.

"Indeed," Carver said. "After a month, the being comes to life to do your bidding. It is very similar to another version of these strange creatures, called the toyol, from your neighboring Malaysia. Interesting, isn't it, how stories and myths can cross oceans and continents? But as I said, there are many ways to generate homunculi, and whoever has created your copies, Dustin, has found an exemplary manner of doing so."

Then all of those doppelgangers, all my clones had come from the same source. That shouldn't have been at all surprising. They had the same objective, after all, of stealing magical items. The Heartstopper, Madam Chien's jade peach, the Null Dagger – it didn't matter what they went for, did it?

"I think it's safe to say that Thea is behind this," I said. "But why is she sending all of these creatures out to steal artifacts? And how did she get my blood?"

Carver stroked his chin. "It's possible that she kept a sample when she first sacrificed you. But the more likely possibility is that she collected one during your last encounter. When you fought Thea, did she cut you at all? Think."

I stared off into empty space as my mind ticked through our last battle. "She did. She slashed me with her talons. You don't mean to say that she managed to keep enough of my blood just from one cut?"

"The woman is a powerful sorceress and an accomplished enchantress. To say that she also has a firm grasp on alchemy wouldn't be a stretch. She didn't need much of your blood to work with. Whatever she harvested from you that one night was more than enough. As for why she's stealing artifacts – that remains a mystery. Sterling?"

Sterling grunted.

"Perhaps you could speak with Diaz."

"Are we talking about the blood witch?" I said. "The one who sent two vampires to corner me in a dark alley?" I frowned a little, remembering that I still hadn't managed to make time for a burger.

"I would be quite upset if someone stole my enchantments as well," Carver said, "but I confess that Diaz's actions were somewhat rash. I am unable to locate Thea because of her cloaking mechanisms, but perhaps Diaz has his own way of tracing the homunculi back to their point of origin."

"Or," Sterling said, grinning, "or, we could start from the source." He winked at me. "I might be able to track them down. But I'd need another taste to be sure."

"Sterling," I groaned. "No. Stop."

"You're right," Sterling said, rising from the table, stretching his limbs and yawning, like a cat. "We may as well go with someone who knows his stuff. Let me take a nap, then I'll contact Diaz for a meeting."

"Dustin should come," Carver added.

"Oh. I should? Yay."

Sterling chuckled. "It'll be fun. Diaz is okay. The twelve vampires he lives with, though? Not so much."

My eyes went straight for the pantry, where we kept all the garlic. If only they were afraid of the stuff.

I pulled out my phone, wondering where in Valero I could go to buy myself a stake. Just — just in case.

Chapter 15

"So you cleared this with Carver, right?"

I sipped on my latte, eyeing Herald with a little more guilt than I'd intended to show.

"Um, yeah. Sure. Sure I did."

Herald nudged his glasses up his nose, fixing me with a quick scowl before turning his attention back to the road. "You're a terrible liar, Graves."

"Actually I'm usually really good at it. You just happen to be really good at sniffing me out."

"What a pair we make," Herald muttered. I could hear his eyes rolling. "But seriously. This sounds like the exact kind of thing Carver would have your head for."

This was true. Sterling said he needed a nap, and besides, he hadn't clarified whether we were going to see Diaz that very same day, so I made plans. It had taken some hemming and hawing on my part, but after hours of pacing back and forth in my bedroom I finally gathered up the balls to pick up the phone and call Herald. And even then we had to swing by for coffees to help settle my jitters. I realize that sounds totally counterintuitive, but just go with it.

I told him I would pay him back for the car rental. I guess I could have gone on my own, but I didn't know how to drive. Okay, fine, I do, but I was too anxious to do it. Plus the destination was on the edge of town, and unfamiliar to me. I didn't want to go it on my own.

I hear you, okay? Yes, I could have taken a rideshare. Enough already. Maybe I was nervous. I hadn't seen my dad in ages, and I needed the moral support.

A stupid idea, you say? Totally. Sure. For the record, you and Herald are on the same page. But I couldn't deal with it anymore. Arachne had given me his address. I'd been through more life-threatening scrapes in the past few months than I have in my entire existence. And I knew that the danger was only going to amp up.

Some sinister shit was going on behind this whole homunculus business, and someone was going to get hurt real bad. I wanted to see my dad just in case. It'd be the first time in a long while. If things went truly horribly for me somehow, between the meeting with Diaz's vampires and the unknowable threat of the doppelgangers, it might even be the last.

"Carver doesn't have to find out, okay? And he won't. Not unless you rat me out to him."

"I won't," Herald harrumphed. "It's not like we're hanging in some secret group chat together. What, I'll be like, 'Hey Carver, your boy Dustin is out here making awesome life choices again.'"

"Don't be a dick, Herald, this is hard enough as it is."

He scoffed. "Speaking as a member of the Lorica, I want you to know that this is highly irresponsible, and a direct violation of the Veil." Then Herald sighed. "But speaking as your friend? I understand why you want to do this. And I support you."

I smiled at him. "Thanks, man."

"No problem," Herald said, brushing his hair out of his eyes, giving me a rare smile in return. He drove on, and I waited for the followup. "It'll only cost you a steak dinner."

Ah. There it was. "Whatever you want, buddy. Anything you like." And I suppose I was thankful for the shift in scenery, because it meant a change in subject as well. "I think we're almost here."

The vegetation was thinning. We'd passed a whole lot of nothing in the course of finding my father's new home. I wouldn't exactly say we were out in the boonies, but saying it was the edge of town might have undersold the distance. We definitely weren't in Valero anymore. Things were getting pretty rural, and the shift from a bunch of trees to actual buildings was a welcome sight.

"We're almost here," Herald said, tapping his phone. "We just have to make a right turn, and –"

"Yikes."

"Oh," Herald said. "Oh wow."

I didn't know whether Herald was seeing the same thing I was, but it wouldn't have mattered. All the houses looked about the same, each in a more or less similar state of disrepair. What was once white was weathered, lawns untended, and shingles? What shingles? I had to admit, I was surprised that any of these houses were even on a GPS map.

My heart did a little tumble. Dad lived in one of these things. I should have guessed that his mental health would have taken even more of a nosedive all this time after my death. I should have come to see him sooner.

But it was going to be okay. We were going to get together again, on better terms, this time, and I was going to do what I could to move him back into the city, get him back on his feet. Maybe he could even reapply for his old job. We could be a family again.

"Color me crazy," Herald said, "but it kind of looks like nobody lives around here."

"I believe you. Half these places look almost abandoned. Which one is he in again?"

"Number forty-two. That one, on the left."

It looked like every other house, except that it seemed slightly more maintained. The porch was still as busted as any other, floored over with uneven wood, the beams scarred with chipping paint, the railings grown over with weeds. The setting sun only made it look all the more forlorn. I had to get him out of there, and soon.

"This is it," I said.

The engine sputtered to a halt. Herald tapped the steering wheel twice, as if with some finality. "Yeah. This is it. Get out there and make me proud."

"Wait, you're not coming with me?"

"What are you, Dustin? Twelve years old?"

I batted my eyelashes. I don't know, don't judge me. Like I said, the whole point of taking Herald with me was for moral support.

"Fine," Herald growled. "Fucking fine. You're such a baby."

"Thanks, man." I scrambled out of the car. "You're the best."

Herald did what I thought was his best not to slam the car door too hard. "Huge, fucking baby."

My feet carried me to the porch, and I had to admonish them mentally. Not too fast. We'd waited months already, I thought. Another minute more wouldn't make much difference. I stood at the threshold, breathing slowly, checking in with myself. This was it. I looked over my shoulder. Herald stood there expectantly, arms crossed, lip turned up, as supportive as he'd ever be.

"Go on," he said, but not unkindly. "I'll be right here if you need me."

"Thanks," I muttered, more jittery than I'd hoped. I turned to the door, lifting my hand for the knob –

Which was when I noticed that the door was ajar.

"Huh," I said. "Funny. It's already open."

Herald peered over my shoulder. "Maybe he left it open. Maybe he was carrying stuff from the car and forgot."

I craned my neck over to the side of the house, where my dad's beat-up old sedan was parked. Both the doors and the trunk were shut.

"Something like that, probably," I told Herald. But something unsettling stirred in the pit of my stomach. It wasn't like dad to leave the front door open.

I cracked it further open, just to test. Everything seemed mostly normal. The lights in the living room were on. There were boxes on the floor, still unpacked, gone dusty from being untouched. A brown plant sat in the corner, untended and unwatered.

Beyond the plant, on the kitchen tile, lay the body of Norman Graves.

Chapter 16

"Dad. Dad?"

I don't think I've ever moved so fast in my entire life. I bolted to his side, the tile cold against my knees even through the denim. What the hell was I supposed to do? I cradled his head, without even knowing if that was okay. I swept the hair away from his brow, because it was all I could do.

"Am I allowed to do this? Herald, am I supposed to do this?" I wasn't sure when my voice started cracking. It became a little harder to see Herald, which was when I realized that the tears were starting to flow.

Herald knelt by me, his hand going to dad's neck, over his chest, under his nose.

"He's alive," Herald said. "He's alive, Dust,

don't worry. Your father's going to be okay."

"Who could have done this?" The door was ajar. A robber? Who the hell would come to a dump of a community like this and think there was anything worth stealing in a ten-mile radius? A junkie, maybe. Someone desperate or drugged-up enough to break into someone's house and steal their shit. "Who would do this to him?" I demanded, as if Herald would have any answers.

"Calm down, Dust. Let me focus. It's going to be okay."

I shut up when I noticed what he was doing, when I saw the filaments of purple light trailing from his fingers. There was no telling what all Herald had in his compendium of spells, but instinctively I knew he was doing his best to cast healing magic over my father. I could have hugged Herald right then and there. I could have bought him two whole steak dinners.

Tendrils of violet light danced over my father's body, curling against his skin. What it was doing, exactly, I couldn't tell, but it was enough to get him conscious again. Dad moaned softly, finally stirring. Herald kept up his spell, his incanting finally ended. He turned to me and gave me a tight smile.

"He's going to be okay, Dust."

I nodded, then stroked my father's forehead. "You're going to be okay, dad. You hear that? You're going to be fine."

He stirred then, his head turning to follow the

weight of my hand.

"Hmm," he murmured. "Dust?"

"Dad?" Something like fire lit up in my chest. My smile must have burned like the sun. "It's me, dad. It's me."

"It's me, dad."

It was another voice. I could have convinced myself that it was an echo, because I recognized the voice as my own.

"Oh God, Dust," Herald said. "Holy fuck."

I looked down the same direction he was staring, down the same corridor, to find my own face leering back at me.

"It's me, dad," the thing in the hallway said. "It's me."

I snarled. "I'll fucking kill you."

I didn't even have to think to tell my body to move. Instinct did it all for me. I rushed the homunculus, with no plan in mind, whether to strike it, or burn it, or slash it with a blade from out of the Dark. I just caught a glimpse of its grin before it turned tail and bolted, smashing into the front door with its shoulder and throwing it open. That only made me want to hurt it more.

Somewhere behind me I vaguely registered Herald shouting for me to stop, but I didn't. I couldn't, I realized, and I didn't want to. All that mattered was for me to put an end to the homunculus, to end this creature that had fucking dared to put a hand on my father.

It was dark out. Night had fallen, and

whatever else the creature was, it was cunning, sprinting straight into the woods near the community. I ran after it, keeping my eyes focused on the pallor of its skin, and on the strange glimmer of red that shone from somewhere inside its hand. Had these things learned to use magic? Was it an artifact? Didn't matter. I wanted it dead.

My lungs heaved. I skidded to a stop, the dry, dead leaves carpeting the earth rustling as my shoes disturbed them.

I stalked through the darkness, the starlight showing that there was nothing around me but trees. That, and more dead leaves, and dirt, and dry twigs that snapped underfoot. I knew it was stupid, giving myself away like that, but I was far too angry. Then something dropped out of the night and threw me to the ground, knocking the air clear out of my lungs.

The homunculus straddled my chest, grabbing me by the lapels and slamming me into the earth. Every blow pushed more of my breath out of me, and as soft as the ground was the creature still assaulted me with enough strength to leave me weak, winded.

The thing at the warehouse had come at me from behind, from out of the darkness. It knew my moves, how I liked to attack. And this one dropped on me from out of a tree, the way I'd recently learned to literally get the drop on my enemies. It was clever. It had my memories.

Its fist slammed into my jaw, and I grunted, tasting blood. So it also liked to punch. It struck again, this time with its other hand. Something rattled and clinked as cold, serrated metal cut into my cheek. It was the chain of an amulet. The red glow from the thing's hand was the garnet set into a verdigris pendant.

A verdigris amulet. Where did the homunculus get that? It attacked dad. Which meant –

The homunculus raised its fist, its breathing labored from the effort, and from the soft laughter it issued each time it struck. It poised to punch again just as I thrust my arm out, slamming my open hand against its face.

I summoned the flames.

The homunculus reared back, shrieking as amber fire burst from the palm of my hand. Maybe I didn't understand the physics and arcane intricacies of throwing fireballs yet, but that didn't mean I couldn't fuck something up by touching it. The creature broke away from me, scrabbling across the ground. The joy of burning the thing, the sheer ecstasy of incineration swelled in my chest, singing like a battle cry.

The confusion was all I needed. I couldn't tell you how I truly felt to see my own face consumed by flames. Half of it was charred, melted, the other half still grinning and leering at me with its remaining black eye. It was taunting me. I leapt for its throat. We both came crashing to the ground, but this time, I was on top.

"You can come for me all you want. But you do not come for my family."

"My family," the thing burbled through its half-ruined mouth. "My family."

"You do not. Hurt. My family." Each time I paused, I struck the homunculus in the face. Each blow ruined it more, twisted the same features I saw each time I looked in the mirror. And with each punch, the thing underneath me quaked, and groaned, and laughed.

"My family," it gurgled.

I grasped it by the throat, pressing my thumb far too hard against where its voice box would be. The thing gasped, then chortled. This was it. I'd been made into something that was now only half human, and that other side of me that was something else, that was other, it longed to rear its head.

The craving for violence felt far too familiar. The Dark Room's occupants rallied behind the scar in my chest, frothing and fighting to escape so that they could rend, and flay, and smother. And when they dealt the killing blow, I knew I would feel their same grisly satisfaction.

"I'll send you to hell," I sputtered through gritted teeth, my grip tightening around the thing's neck. "Then I'll find Thea. I'll find your mother, and I'll kill her."

I'll kill her, I thought, my insides blooming with preemptive delight. I'll fucking kill her.

"Mother," the thing laughed. "Mother."

Something in me knew to stop choking the homunculus, to ease the pressure on its throat long enough to let it get some air down, to let it breathe – and to let it believe for long enough that I was going to allow it to live. My scar burned as I lifted my head to the stars, as I searched the night sky for the last traces of my humanity, of mercy.

A glorious warmth spilled down my chin as the wound raked into my cheek bled freely. It was the price that the Dark Room demanded each time I brought it into our world from out of the gloom. And with the woods around me plunged into shadow, the stage was set for my impostor's absolute evisceration.

I hissed at the pain and pleasure of my wound opening and bleeding. Six huge spikes burst from the ground, gleaming and velvet-black, solid blades of shadow sent from the Dark itself. I felt the warmth of flesh as they pierced the homunculus through its limbs, its chest, its throat. I felt every rivulet of its artificial blood as it ran down the spears and spines that were as much a part of the Dark Room as they were an extension of me. The warmth brought me comfort. The warmth brought me rapture.

The homunculus shuddered, choking and gurgling its last. Then it went still. I curled my fingers through the dead thing's hair, staring into the scorched face of the brother I had slain. This was better than sex. It was better than redemption. Nothing in that moment could have pleased me more.

I watched as the homunculus dissolved into gore, as the red-rust slime of its body seeped into the earth. I threw my head back and sipped in the night air, clawing at my chest, fighting to keep down the howl that threatened to escaped my throat.

I raked at my hair, thrumming from the pleasure of the kill. The stars sang to me as they watched. The stars whispered. Murderer, they called me. Sinner. I dared to look back at the stars, and from deep inside of me, I laughed.

Chapter 17

"Sit still," Herald grumbled.

I winced at his touch. He was a lot cruder than Asher, tugging on my jaw to align it as he cast his spell, but beggars can't be choosers. My cheek still fucking hurt, and I was happy to take all the restorative magic I could get. He frowned harder, pulling on my jaw roughly when I accidentally let my head loll off to the side.

"Fucking ouch," I mumbled. "Your bedside manner needs some serious work, Igarashi."

"So do your fighting skills, but you don't see me bitching about them." He smirked. "Oh wait. I just did."

Dad looked between us open-mouthed as purple tendrils of energy surged from Herald's skin to mine, probing my body on a cellular level to stitch together the shallow, torn flesh in my cut.

"Will someone please tell me what's going on?" he croaked.

"Where to start?" Herald said, his eyes turned up to the ceiling. "Let's see. A psychotic sorceress faked your son's death, thereby triggering his latent arcane abilities. He turned into a kind of magical sneak thief – not a criminal, mind you, he works on the side of good. Well, mostly. And now he fights evil on a regular basis, including the thing that attacked and knocked you out." He pushed his glasses up his nose, watching me with more than a little smugness. "That about enough to bring him up to speed?"

"More or less," I grumbled. I gave dad a tight smile. "That sums it up. This is my job now. Mainly it's to secure enchanted artifacts so that my boss – this immortal wizard guy – can research them and make sure they stay out of the wrong hands. I live in a pocket dimension with a werewolf and a vampire. Also a Filipino dude who happens to be a necromancer."

Dad stared at me mouth agape, his forehead knitted into bewildered creases.

Herald sighed. "Easiest way is to show him, Dust."

I shrugged. This was the second time I was asked to show off my talents in as many days, but lest we forget, I'm totally okay with being the center of attention. And if it meant helping my dad understand my new situation, well, so much the better.

"Dad? Don't freak out, okay? I'm about to show you what I can do."

He lifted a finger. "Hold that thought." He turned for the fridge, pulled out a beer, somehow snapped off the top with his bare hand, and took a long, delicious pull. He slammed the bottle on the counter, half of it already gone, then nodded. "Okay. I think I'm ready. Wait. Probably not, but I don't really have much choice, do I?"

I smiled and shook my head. "Here goes."

This was second nature by now, and the shortness of my jaunt meant that it was as easy as breathing or blinking. I melted into my own shadow on the ground, the top of my head sinking into the floor just as I heard my father gasping.

I did a brisk jog through the Dark Room, following the pinpoint of light that I knew would bring me over to the shadow by the refrigerator. I emerged there, the fridge humming quietly beside me, then cleared my throat.

Dad's mouth hung open in shock over my disappearance. He gave off a noise somewhere between a grunt and a yelp. His eyes flitted from my hair to my feet, then back again. Shaking his head, dad lifted his beer to his mouth and tossed back the rest of it.

"Wow," I said. "You need to control your drinking a little bit."

Dad ran the back of his hand across his lips, then rubbed it on his shirt. "Depending on where this is going, I might actually start drinking even more."

"Dad, c'mon."

"Bad joke. I'm sorry." He clasped his hands together, pushing his knuckles into his forehead, before he looked at me again, studying me for a moment. "So this is who you are now? This is what you do?"

I shrugged and tried on a little smile. "Hey. It's a living." I stared at my thumb. "You're not mad, are you?"

He frowned. "All these months I thought you were dead. You've got friends, a job, a home. I couldn't be happier. I won't pretend to fully understand what you do, but I'm proud of you." He cleared the room in two strides, looking as big as he did when I was a child, like someone who would always take care of me. He wrapped his arms around me, cuffing one hand behind my neck, and pulled tight. "I can't believe you're back, Dust. I thought I lost my son. I couldn't be luckier. I love you."

I squeezed back, feeling smaller, letting myself be enveloped in the warmth of the only parent I had left. God but I didn't know how much I'd missed being around him. I choked out a little laugh, fighting to stifle the sob in my throat.

"Love you too, dad."

He stepped back, clapping me by the

shoulders, then fixed me with the same blue eyes that I saw every time I looked in the mirror. "I don't know what you are, exactly, but I'm proud of you."

I ran a finger under my eye, sniffled, then chuckled. "I'm not sure what I am, either, but I think it has something to do with this thing that mom left behind."

I pulled the amulet out of my pocket, lifting it up to our faces. The pendant spun on its axis, the garnet glinting like a red eye. Across the room, Herald folded his arms, watching the amulet intensely.

Dad made a face, his lips pursing, as if he'd just tasted something awful. "She was attached to that thing, but it always creeped me the hell out. Didn't know why she kept it around. It has no value, as far as we've checked. It's just as cheap and worthless as the others."

The stifling silence from Herald's end of the room made me look. His eyes were burning into me with grim understanding. I watched dad warily.

"The – the others, you say?"

"I only held onto them as keepsakes, but I have them tucked under the bed. Never look at them, you know? Like I said. It all freaks me out. Something about the way they're designed. All those curls, they look like tentacles. Like squid or something."

Like shrikes, like the children of the Eldest. I

avoided Herald's gaze, but I could basically hear his thoughts.

"Where are the rest of these objects, Mr. Graves?" Herald said, his voice level and artificially professional.

Dad looked between us, his face a mix of confusion and suspicion. "I'll just go and grab them," he said, heading to his bedroom.

I rushed to Herald's side as dad sauntered off. Herald tugged on my wrist just as soon as we were in whispering range, his face conspiratorially close to mine.

"These artifacts belong to the Eldest and their servants. Where the hell would your mother get them?"

"How the fuck would I know?" I growled. "This is the first we're both hearing of this."

"This is bad," Herald said, glowering. "First order of business is for us to remove them from the premises. I sense no enchantment on the amulet, but I can't say the same for the others."

"But the homunculus came specifically for the amulet. So it isn't enchanted. Fine. It still gave off a signature strong enough to attract the creature."

"Even more reason for us to remove the entire lot," Herald said. "It sounds like Norman wouldn't mind very much. He doesn't seem attached to them. They'll be safe back with the Lorica."

My eyes narrowed. "Or," I said, very evenly,

"or at the Boneyard."

Herald cocked an eyebrow. "The what now?"

"Shush. We'll talk about this later. Here he comes."

Dad was balancing a box in his arms. Not just a box, actually, but a proper wooden chest, about the size of a shoebox. It looked a little weathered, and unremarkable apart from the meaningless, generic designs carved into its lid and its sides.

Yet even without any real training for sensing the presence of magical objects, I could detect something sinister about the chest. It was that unsettling, uncomfortable feeling you get when something's off, even if you don't know what that something might specifically be.

I watched in trepidation as dad set the chest down on the kitchen table. Herald leaned closer, arms folded, like he was dying to know himself. Dad lifted the lid, and I held my breath.

It was a whole lot of nothing. Just junk: dented pieces of metal, broken jewelry, the pommel of a dagger with its whole blade missing, and something that looked like a metal chopstick. What did bind the objects together, though, was that all of them were made of tarnished bronze, in that same, strange verdigris color as the sacrificial daggers, as Vanitas. Here and there, I caught the dull, lifeless glimmer of dusty, long-hidden garnets.

"These things are functionally worthless," Herald said, casting a professional eye over the contents of the box. One hand nudged at his spectacles, as if to afford him a better look. "They might have been enchanted once, but right now? Nothing. Still, even as junk, they give off enough of an energy signature, which explains why the homunculus came here."

Dad sighed and clapped one hand on Herald's shoulder. Herald looked abashed by the gesture, or perhaps by the sudden contact.

"Listen," dad said. "You seem like a nice kid, but for all I know you may as well be speaking French."

"I'm. I'm Japanese," Herald stammered.

"Not the point, Herald. Dad? The thing that attacked you, it's called a homunculus, and there's a lot of them wandering out in the city right now. We're trying to figure out why, but all we know is that they're attracted to magical items."

Dad raised an eyebrow, then picked up one of the verdigris objects. "This garbage is magical? It was just old junk your mom kept around."

"Yes, well, about that," Herald said, having collected himself. "We'll need to remove these from your home to protect you. More homunculi might come for them if we don't." Herald nodded at me. "For that matter, we might have to set other protections in place."

He was going to ward dad's house? Oh, man. Herald deserved three steak dinners. I smiled at him, hoping it was enough to convey my thanks.

"But I hope you don't mind me asking, Mr. Graves. Where did your wife acquire these? They're quite rare, and frankly speaking, quite dangerous."

"My wife had a thing for strange knick-knacks, see. She never really put much stock in them, but she liked to tinker, keep them around. I never thought much of it. I mean, how could a crystal really hurt you? But this box?" He tapped the side of the chest. "It was a long time ago. Someone sold it to her for basically nothing, this lady she met on one of those occult message boards. Blond woman, had kind of an odd name. Thay – something. Theya?"

My fist shook, and my nails dug into the palm of my hand. Herald looked at me, then back at my dad.

"Mr. Graves. Was it someone named Thea Morgana?"

Dad put down the pommel, then blinked.

"How could you possibly know?"

Chapter 18

Herald circled the house a third time, drawing a line on the ground with pinches of something from a little jar. It turned out to be a barbecue rub that dad had lying around. Herald muttered as he went, sprinkling the earth with something that would have gone nicely on a slab of ribs.

Dad looked on in suspicion. "Seems like a waste."

"Shush," I said. "And when were you going to barbecue around here, anyway? This place looks dead. I don't think you even have any neighbors."

"Oh, they're around," he said, looking at the other houses. "They just keep to themselves is all."

Night had fallen, and it was a little strange how so few of the surrounding houses had any lights on at all. I guess I could begin to understand why dad liked it. It was a place for him to hide, to be away from everyone and everything, but especially his thoughts and his past. But it was time to change that.

"This is a temporary measure, you realize?" I said, gesturing at Herald. "He's casting wards, but you're going to have to move back to the city soon."

The corner of dad's mouth lifted, the bristly mustache he'd grown over the months lifting with it. "You miss me that much?"

I chucked him on the shoulder. "Stop being so sappy. But yes. Besides, I'd feel safer with you nearby. You don't know how dangerous shit gets for me sometimes, and I'd be happier knowing we won't have to drive out to bumfuck nowhere just to check on you."

"I'll be fine until then," he said reassuringly. Then he jabbed his thumb at Herald again. "Though I don't know if all this is necessary. Especially that. Now that seems like a waste."

Herald was emptying an entire bottle of beer over the patch of dirt right across the front door. I had no idea what the hell he was doing, but I trusted him implicitly. I'd always known he was a proficient sorcerer, and knowing that Carver held him in high regard deepened that trust even more. Plus who was I to argue with an alchemist? If he thought that barbecue rub was the best thing for drawing a magical perimeter, then who was I to say otherwise?

Herald dropped the bottle. It fell to the earth with a soft thud. He stopped incanting, then snapped his fingers. Dad gasped, stepped away from the house, and grabbed at my arm.

"Holy shit," he said, the brilliant purple of so many flames reflected in his eyes.

"I know," I said, turning my attention to the ring of violet fire that had sprung up around his house. "I know."

The fires subsided in a matter of seconds, vanishing into the ground, as if called back by the earth. Herald dusted off his hands, a gesture to symbolize that the ritual had ended – or maybe just a way to get rid of the extra rub clinging to his fingers. He thrust the jar into my dad's hands. I could tell he was trying not to smirk at the sight of my dad's face.

"There wasn't any sage in the house," Herald said. "I had to make do. The beer cements the connection to the earth. Wheat and spring water, and all that."

I raised an eyebrow. "What, really?"

Herald shrugged. "I dunno. Sure, why not. Listen, the point is, this will offer some preliminary protection, and a kind of early detection system. You'll find out if something's wrong with Norman here."

Dad frowned. "Hey now. I can take care of myself."

I cleared my throat. "Just like you took care of

yourself when the homunculus clocked you in the back of the head? No way. We're not taking any risks."

Dad grumbled.

"But Herald, you were saying. An alarm? I mean, how would I even know?"

The circle of protection he'd drawn around the house flared purple once again, the briefest flash of light, and a siren began screaming in my head. I groaned and clutched at my temples.

"Kind of like that," Herald said, frowning. He put his hand across dad's chest, already incanting. In his other hand, razor-sharp fragments of ice were starting to form, growing in size by the second.

I straightened myself up, willing the noise away. I guess I'd get used to it, but I'd have to ask Herald if there was some way of adjusting the hellish volume on that thing. But before that, we needed to deal with whatever threat was setting off the occult security system in the first place. I readied myself, surveying the darkness beyond the house, wondering whether I'd need to resort to flame or shadow.

But it wasn't another homunculus. The shape that appeared from out of the shadows was familiar, except she wasn't. I knew her face, or perhaps I didn't, because her features kept shifting. Yet even as her form wavered, I knew that I recognized something about the woman, about her cloak of shadows, her head of raven-black hair that seemed to melt into the night.

Hecate.

"Holy shit," Herald murmured. "Holy shit, it's really her." He dropped his hand, the icicles evaporating into thin air, and he lowered his head, as if in reverence.

Dad nudged me with his elbow. "Is – is that a vampire?"

"Not quite," I said. "Possibly worse. I think it's best if you go into the house and wait there."

He frowned. "Okay, Dust, I appreciate what you and your buddy here have done to help me, but I swear I can take care of myself. Your father isn't as defenseless as you think he is and – "

"Dad. Please." I leaned in, my eyes watching as Hecate slowly approached. "It's a goddess. And it's not one of the nicer ones."

His eyes widened. "Did you say – that's a goddess? They exist?"

I pressed my lips into a tight line. "There's a hell of a lot we need to catch up on. But for now, please get into the house."

"Take care of yourself," he sputtered, shortly before bolting through the front door. I'd never seen him move so fast.

"Goodness gracious," Hecate said, holding a hand to her chest, as if in mock offense. "We did not come to harm your parent, fleshling. There was no need to dismiss him so. We have come with other interests in mind."

"Well and good, Hecate," I said. "But he's only

just learning about the arcane and the entities. I think he's seen quite enough for one night."

She tilted her head and smiled. "How sweet of you to be so concerned for your father's sanity. The human mind truly is such a fragile thing." She turned her head slowly. "But we see that another fleshling is content to remain within our presence."

"Herald Igarashi," Herald said, bowing his head again. I'd never seen him like this, cowed, perhaps, and so restrained, because I could tell he was getting a little excited. "I'm a huge fan of your work," he added.

Hecate laughed. "We certainly do our best. But first, there is much to discuss." Hecate craned her neck towards dad's house. "We smell the taint of the Old Ones in this home. It was the stockpile of their implements that drew us here. Are we correct in assuming that there is a chest full of enchanted star-metal somewhere in this delicate and extremely flammable shelter?"

"Did you mean the verdigris? Star-metal? Is that what it's called?"

I took her silence to mean "Yes."

"Then okay, you're correct," I said. "And I really wish that you didn't dwell so much on how flammable the place is. I'm already worried enough as it is."

Hecate waved her hand and laughed. "Surely the darkling mage is not so afraid for his father's life that a mere joke is enough to unsettle him?

Surely one who has defeated something as powerful and maniacal as the white witch possesses more spine and grit than that."

The white witch. She was talking about Thea. I said nothing, and just as well, because when Hecate spoke again, it was as if she had read my mind. She had a weird habit of doing that.

"And if our memory serves, this same white witch destroyed a possession of yours. Not a possession, truly, but an ally. A friend." She placed her hand on my cheek, her skin smooth and warm against the chill of the night. "Such a pity to have lost a friend. But we have come to tell you that there is hope. The box of broken treasures your mother left behind may yet be your salvation, fleshling."

Herald's eyes lit up. "It's salvage, isn't it? All that verdigris, that broken bronze, it can be used to help reforge Vanitas."

And that's when my eyes lit up. "Is that true?"

Hecate nodded and withdrew her hand. She moved back, then reappeared several paces away, shadowstepping the way she did when we first met. It always felt as if she'd done so to display some sense of kinship with me and my talent, and now she had come with a way to bring Vanitas back. If Hecate was planning to exact some kind of price, I was afraid to find out what it was, how expensive and debilitating.

She turned her hands up, and out of the darkness glimmered a strange assortment of shapes, like the disparate, unraveled pieces of some grand pattern. "The sword's destruction has diminished its enchantment, and much of its magic was consumed when it was shattered. But now that you've found additional material, there are new possibilities."

She gestured with her hands, and the pale green pinpricks of light rearranged themselves into the outline of a sword. It hovered in the air before me, in very much the same size and shape as Vanitas. An awed sort of sound came from the house. I looked and found my dad standing just behind the front door, peeking through a crack. Hah. Typical. But at least I knew he was safe.

"The only question is, who can we approach to help?" Herald rubbed his chin. "We'd be hard-pressed to find an enchanter talented enough to stitch the sword's magic back together."

"And nor would we ask you to find a mortal to do it," Hecate said. "The qualities of the star-metal that the Old Ones favor for their instruments are detrimental to you fleshlings." She pointed at me. "This one is only unharmed because of the corruption the white witch buried in his heart."

"Wait. Detrimental? Are you saying that just having the verdigris around can be harmful to humans? Like radiation?"

Hecate only looked at me and said nothing. She turned her head towards Herald again before she spoke. "We believe you may need to find an entity powerful enough to undertake this task."

"A god of blacksmiths, perhaps. Hephaestus, maybe?" Herald folded his arms. "Or Kagutsuchi, the Japanese god of fire and forge."

"Clever suggestions," Hecate said, "but we believe that the forge-gods would sooner smite you than entertain the thought of working with the star-metal that carries the taint of the Old Ones. No. This work requires a different sort of entity." She folded her hands together, then lowered her head as she studied Herald with a burning intensity. "Tell us, fleshling. How many of the world's grimoires have you read?"

"As many as I've been able to put my hands on." Herald's face practically glowed with excitement. "Any of the books that have passed through the Lorica. I've seen De Vermis Mysteriis, the Lesser Key of Solomon." He sighed. "One day I'm hoping to get my hands on a copy of the Enchiridion."

"And perhaps, fleshling, one day, a goddess will favor you enough to show you its pages."

Herald's mouth dropped open. "Seriously? Truly? You've read it?"

Hecate ran one hand through her hair, then flipped it nonchalantly over her shoulder. "We wrote it."

I restrained a chuckle. Herald was completely fan-boying over the goddess of magic. The look on his face was so precious that I wish I'd taken a picture.

"What of the Dictionnaire Infernal?" Hecate asked, suddenly serious again. "Have you read it?"

Herald's mouth went tight, a look of distaste passing across his face. "The Infernal Dictionary. I have, yes."

"And are you familiar with the sorts of entities detailed in that tome? Those might be the ones who would be willing to help you."

I threw up my hands. "I have absolutely no idea what either one of you is talking about."

"Those are the names of grimoires, Dust. And the Infernal Dictionary is a compendium of beings from the netherworld. It lists the hierarchy of demons." Herald turned to me with a grave expression. "Hecate wants us to talk to a demon."

Chapter 19

"Make it quick," Herald said, tugging on the handbrake. "I'll wait here. I don't want to risk your roomies spotting me."

"It'll be fine," I said, shrugging on my jacket. "I think you're going to be okay."

I'd asked him to park far enough away from Mama Rosa's Finest Filipino Food, which at least ensured that no one from the Lorica would know where we were based. I also hoped that it stood as a small sign of my fealty to the Boneyard. I mean I trust Herald with my life, but it was the principle of the thing.

"I won't be long," I said.

My heart was pumping. I still wasn't totally comfortable with the idea of taking long shadowsteps, but this was a matter of timing. I needed to get into the Boneyard, somehow avoid running into the other guys, pick up Vanitas's remains, then pop back out and join Herald in the car.

I know what you're thinking. What's the damn rush? On a pragmatic level, the question of so many homunculi appearing in such a short period of time meant that a tidal wave was coming. We were due for a breaking point, and we'd need as many allies as we could muster. Vanitas was as powerful an ally as they came.

But on a more honest note – color me sappy, but I missed the guy. I know this is hard to process, but I think you'd relate if you've ever lost a friend, whether to time, distance, or death. I wanted Vanitas back.

"Here I go," I said, psyching myself up yet again.

"Just fucking go already," Herald snarled, his knuckles white over the steering wheel.

I melded into the darkness inside of the car – which, yes, finding out I could do that was as much a surprise to me as it is to you – and entered the Dark Room. I gauged that the location of the restaurant was at least two blocks away in, um, that direction.

I dashed through the shadows, the vague, blackish tendrils of night sweeping at my cheeks with fond, familiar fingers. When I glimpsed the light at the end of the corridor, I held my breath, shut my eyes tight, and prayed that I wouldn't end up shunted into a brick wall. I took the final step.

The vapors of the Dark Room receded from around me with an audible sigh. I could hear a familiar humming from nearby. I patted at my face, my torso, and my junk, just to make sure that everything was still in place, then finally allowed myself to open my eyes.

The industrial refrigerator in Mama Rosa's kitchen greeted me with its dead, stainless steel face. I'd made it, and with way more accuracy than I'd hoped. I stifled the whoop of delight building in my throat and sidestepped to the left, putting myself in front of the brick wall that concealed Carver's portal.

Damn. I forgot to pack a sharp object on me. I briefly considered picking up a knife from the kitchen to expedite the process, but let's be real, that's totally unhygienic. Mama Rosa's restaurant was a front, sure, but it was still a legitimate business, with regular customers and all. As much as Mama Rosa's dinuguan – a dish made from pig's blood – was a hit, I was pretty sure none of her clients, nor the health inspector, for that matter, would be too pleased to find my blood in the mix.

I placed the fine web of skin between my thumb and forefinger right underneath my canines and bit as hard as I could. I teared a little at the momentary pain, tasting blood, then retrieved just a spot of it to daub over the brick.

I sucked at my skin, feeling the pain fade in intensity, once again faintly jealous of how Herald and Bastion could so conveniently conjure knives from the ethers. I suppose I could have called for a blade from the Dark, but that would have been total overkill.

The Boneyard's portal buzzed into life, a swirling oval of humming amber energy. I stepped in, then ran as quickly and as silently as I could through the flickering flame-lit corridors of the stone temple. I had to pass Gil and Sterling's doors to get to my own room, but both were mercifully shut. Gil was probably out with Prudence, and Sterling was probably hunting for a meal.

I dashed into my bedroom, grabbing the enchanted knapsack Herald had gifted me from the Gallery, the one that could hold more than it looked because its inside was an entire pocket dimension. I swept the busted bronze and shattered garnets of Vanitas's body into the bag, hefted it over my shoulder, and started to run out of my bedroom. A body blocked the exit, and I bit my tongue to hold back a yelp of surprise.

It was Asher, barefoot and dressed in a tank top and striped pajamas, his hair a tousled mess. He rubbed blearily at one eye and stared curiously at me out of the other.

"I heard noises," he mumbled.

"Just me," I said. "Go on back to sleep. Everything's fine."

He scratched his belly. "Sterling says we're gonna go meet a bunch of vampires soon."

That's right. The meeting with Diaz and his cohorts. See, that was an even more compelling reason to get the business of reforging Vanitas over and done with. A sword, at the end of the day, is just a really sharp and pointy stake. And the only thing better than a stake is a rocket-powered homing stake that can stab and destroy things on its own.

"We'll meet them soon. Real soon." I patted him on the shoulder. "Go back to bed. And Asher? You didn't see me."

He gave me a limp smile and two thumbs up, waddled into his bedroom, then shut the door, which was when I realized something. He said "we" when he mentioned the meeting with Diaz, didn't he? So Asher was coming along? Surely Carver knew.

I raced out of my own bedroom. There was no sign of Carver just yet, which was only making me increasingly antsy. I pulled tighter on my knapsack's straps and made a beeline for the portal.

Where Carver was waiting.

"Dustin," he said, his voice calm, cool, and suspiciously neutral.

"Hi. Hey. Sup." I smoothed a hand through my hair, meaning to play things casual. Nothing to see here, just another totally normal night of me running through the halls with a magical backpack strapped to my shoulders.

"I am not entirely sure what you're up to, but I trust that you've got your head on right."

"I, um, sure." Don't look to the left, I told myself. Or – or was it the right? I'd read somewhere that it was how human lie detectors could tell that you were fibbing. I stared straight into Carver's eyes, in total denial of the fact that he didn't need to learn how to read body language and facial tics to figure that out. He was a walking radar and surveillance array. I don't think I've ever successfully snuck anything past him in the months we'd known each other. At least not for long.

He rubbed his chin, shook his head, and sighed. "Whatever it is you have planned – please don't let it end in disaster. But you're a grown man, and I cannot say that I'm disappointed in your magical progress, between your new taste for fire, and your finer control over your shadow blades."

I wasn't expecting compliments. I never expected compliments from Carver. I kept my voice steady. "Right," I said.

"Just come home in one piece. And about reforging the sword. We may have to look beyond gods for now. I'll inform you if I find a suitable candidate."

"Actually," I said, my mouth oddly dry. "I might just go in the other direction for help. Hecate told me to consider speaking to a – um, a demon."

Carver studied me for a strained, quiet moment. He took so long to speak that I had to wonder if he thought it was a terrible idea. I considered sprinting for the portal before he tried restraining me, but he angled his head to the side, then spoke.

"I cannot believe I am saying this but – that might just work. I confess, it's an angle that I hadn't considered. Though I trust you'll be mindful to take extreme care with the negotiations." His eyes narrowed as he walked past me, back into the hallway leading to his office. "Gods may be fickle and obtuse, but demons are far, far worse. Try not to agree to terms that will destroy the world as we know it. There is still so much I want to do."

"Right," I said to his back. "Check. No apocalypses."

Carver stopped in his tracks, but didn't turn. "Oh, and Dustin? Send your father my regards."

I froze. Ah. I knew that he'd sniffed something out. Still, I couldn't help but smile. "I will, Carver. And thanks."

I ran back through the portal, then leapt into the shadow of the refrigerator in the kitchen, even more amped up about the communion Herald and I were about to perform. This was a different kind of Carver. I didn't know if he was treating me differently because he'd shown me so much more of himself, if this was a gesture of trust on his part.

My chest might have puffed up a little as I hurried through the Dark Room. For once, Carver felt comfortable enough to let me wear the big boy pants. The best I could hope for was to not royally fuck this all up.

Lowering my head, I ran straight for the heart of the light at the end of the Dark Room's tunnel, bolting like a bullet through the darkness. The plan was to exit right where I'd first entered.

And bam. The ethers parted, and I landed butt-first in the passenger seat, next to a slightly upset and mildly pallid Herald.

"Jesus H. Christ, Dustin! What the hell, man. Don't do that."

I folded my hands behind my head and grinned. "Do what?"

"You're a little shithead," he grumbled, gripping the steering wheel tight. "Did you get the goods?"

"Right here."

I patted at my backpack, comforted by the worn but somehow buttery-soft leather of it. I missed having this thing on my back, because wearing it generally meant that I was carrying Vanitas around inside. After tonight, if all went well, things might go back to the way they were. It almost didn't bother me knowing that we still had to suck up to a full-blown, actual demon.

"So," I said. "Off to the tether."

"I'm on it." Herald adjusted the map on his

phone. "It's near a bank in a slightly jankier part of the business district. So not all that far from the Lorica."

"You navigate," I said, "and I'll get our shit ready."

I reached into the backseat, gingerly lifting up the wooden chest filled with mismatched pieces of verdigris. I settled the chest into the bag's pocket dimension. The back of my hand brushing against the cold, jagged edge of a broken garnet.

Soon, V, I thought, patting the jewels and twisted bronze the way I'd pat an old friend on the back. Very soon.

Chapter 20

The tether was a busted ATM stuck in the back of an old building, what a quick search on the internet told us used to be a bank. I watched the eerie blue glow of the machine's grimy, disused screen, peering back at me like a sad, old face.

This was far too fishy, even for all the supernatural weirdness I'd already experienced in the arcane underground. The back alley that we were in was creepy enough without the added oddity of the near-total darkness shrouding the building.

Something about the quality of the shadows told me they were artificial, as if left there for the benefit of some entity that loved to hide in the darkest corners of the earth. And yes, you're right, being surrounded by so much darkness should have been comforting to me, but it wasn't. That wasn't the right kind of dark. It wasn't the kind of gloom that dwelled in the Dark Room, that lived in the world behind my scar.

"Remind me again why we can't hit up one of the gods for this," I muttered.

"Because they won't work with the star-metal. You know that. Kagutsuchi of the Japanese pantheon, or Hadúr of the Hungarian gods, neither will be very pleased if you came to them with that request. Remember when you walked into Amaterasu's realm with Vanitas in your backpack? She didn't seem to like you much then, either. Imagine going up to someone like Hephaestus."

"He singlehandedly forged the weapons of the entire Greek pantheon," I said. "Dude knows his swords."

"And he takes pride in the purity of his work. The very presence of star-metal in his domicile would be a grave offense. He'd smash your head open the moment you walked in."

I glared at the ATM screen, which glared defiantly back, like a single, hazy blue eye. "Isn't there like a fire spirit out there that might want to help?"

"Again. I can't think of any non-god entities that are strong enough to do the job. And again: you've developed kind of a reputation for yourself, and not a great one. Probably best not to piss off more gods for a while. Lay low. They hate you."

"Gee," I said, ruffling my hair in frustration. "Thanks."

Herald gave me a tight smile, then clapped me on the shoulder. "You keep me around because I'm brutally honest, little buddy."

"I'm taller than you."

"And in all honesty? This is probably going to be super dangerous. Come on."

Herald walked up to the ATM, and the sense of foreboding building in my stomach surged even harder than before. He pressed his finger to the screen, which wavered before displaying a series of words.

"Please provide your PIN number," I read out loud.

Herald pushed the number six on the keypad three times. Typical. The screen wavered again, flashing red for the briefest moment, before turning back to blue. New words.

"Please make your deposit."

"The offering," Herald said. "Gimme your wallet."

"Wait, what?"

I cursed as he casually slipped his hand into my back pocket, retrieving my wallet with an enviable measure of grace and finesse. The fucker could probably make as good a thief as me. He was probably even a little faster. And surprisingly strong, I noted, as I tried to take my wallet back.

"Relax," he said, holding it out of reach. He

retrieved the bills, then tossed the wallet back to me. "The machine doesn't want the whole thing. Just your cash."

I fumbled with my wallet, running my fingers mournfully over its worn, weathered creases as I stretched it to peek at its insides. "Really, dude? That's all the cash I have. That's like a good hundred. Come on."

"That's the least of your worries," Herald said, holding the wad of bills up to the screen. They burst into flames. "The demon will probably want more. Much more."

That could have bought me, like, so many cheeseburgers. "You mean the demon wants more money?"

Herald chuckled. "Real cute."

He grabbed my wrist, then pressed my hand up against the screen. I yelped when something sharp shot out of the glass and slashed my finger. I glared at Herald, pulling my hand away. Ouch. I chewed my lip, correctly rethinking the very gross business of sucking at my bloodied finger after it had been in contact with an incredibly grody ATM screen.

"Step back," he said.

I was almost a second too late. The machine writhed and screeched into life. It grew as it warped and folded in upon itself. The seam where it should have spit out cash parted to reveal massive fangs of serrated steel, each bigger and crueler than a kitchen knife.

"Well shit," I muttered, surprised I could hear myself over the agonizing shriek and scrape of rusted metal. The machine had transformed into the gaping maw of some giant beast. I stared warily into the darkness of its throat, and my heart leapt out of my ass when I spotted the first glimmer of fire.

"Oh. Cool. So it's a dragon. No big deal."

Herald wrapped his coat tighter around himself, securing it against the howling wind that blasted from the dragon's throat. "It's a major demon of greed, which means it can afford fancy security systems." The dragon shrieked even louder. "Real fancy ones."

"Oh. Awesome. I thought it was the demon lord of making me shit my fucking pants."

"There's one of those, too, but for now, this is the right address. Come on."

I licked my lips as I watched the flames twirl and dance among the gateway's serrated fangs. "After you," I said.

Herald shrugged, pushed up his glasses, and walked straight into the fire without looking back.

"Thinks he's an action star," I mumbled. I clenched my teeth, and for some inane reason, took a deep breath, filling my lungs with as much air as they could hold. Then I walked into the flames, too.

They were freezing cold, and somehow almost solid as they lapped against my ankles, their chilling touch licking at my shoes. It was like walking into the meat section of a supermarket. Not the frozen goods aisle, exactly, but the bit behind the thick plastic curtains, where they keep all the carcasses.

I'd worked in one of those places once, and as I walked, the smell of charnel and gore returned to me. I steeled myself, expecting the demon's domicile to be exactly as the Abrahamic religions described them: furious, merciless, and filled with the flayed, ruined bodies of sinners.

But as I kept walking, the blaze faded. The gouts of fire disappeared into the ground, which was no longer the same rusted metal of the gateway, but a gleaming marble. The smell of dead animals and spilled blood disappeared, giving way to a distant scent of woodsmoke, citrus, and spice.

In some far, unseen room, a piano played something familiar, or perhaps something forgotten. And instead of the butcher's barrier, in place of the plastic sheets was a grand, gleaming curtain of crimson velvet. Herald was nowhere in sight. I could only assume that he had stepped through, so I ran my hands across the soft, suede-like touch of the curtains, then parted them.

Palatial. That was the only way I could describe the demon's domicile. Sparkling candelabras burned with brilliant fires from their brassy tips, with no candles to be found. Marble so pure and luxurious filled the colossal hallway and its high ceilings with a rich, yet lifeless white. And everywhere, from picture frames and fixtures and chandeliers and statuettes, shone the perpetual radiance of precious gold, a permanent, absolute aura of wealth and excess.

Paintings of strange men and women watched us from every wall. Each was an immensely beautiful specimen, only with a different feature that set them apart from being truly human. Some had the horns of goats and rams. One smiled to show the teeth of a wolf, and another had a patch of scales on its neck so symmetric and radiant that it looked like a collar made of emeralds. But as captivating as the people in the paintings were, nothing compared to the creature that waited for us at the very end of the hall, standing in a pool of molten gold.

Now I'm not the most fashionable person on the planet, but what I could only assume to be a demon wore a suit so finely tailored and so sleekly cut that it looked uncomfortable, almost painful. Its cloth was the gleaming red of rubies, which, I know, how does anyone even pull that off? And the demon's face was harder still to put into words. Regal comes to mind. Noble. Beautiful, terrible, so unearthly that it couldn't possibly be human.

I elbowed Herald gently. "That's the demon?"

He shook his head, giving me a sidelong glance. "Correction. That's the demon prince."

Chapter 21

"Herald Igarashi," the demon said, in a whisper-soft voice that still somehow boomed about the marble corridor. "And Dustin Graves." The demon spread its hands and gave a small bow. "Consider yourselves welcome in the palace of Mammon."

Herald pulled on my jacket, and only then did I realize that I my mouth was hanging open. "Mammon," he whispered. "The demon prince of greed."

Mammon laughed in a voice that was at once as sweet as honey and as ominous as the droning of bees. "And of wealth, and treasure, and infinite riches." The demon beckoned, its spindly fingers tipped with lacquered golden nails. "Come. Let's dispense with the pleasantries. Mammon does not have the luxury of free time."

I whistled as we approached, appraising the massive rubies Mammon wore on each finger, on fine chains around its lily-white throat. "I'd have thought that you'd be all about luxury."

Mammon laughed again, spreading a pair of perfectly manicured hands. "Flattery will get you everywhere, oh thing of shadows. And it will get you everything." Mammon's heart-shaped lips lifted into a smile. "For the right price."

Herald nudged me. "Bring it out. Time for show and tell."

Mammon snapped its fingers and an ornate, lacquered table blinked into existence. "Your sword, correct? It requires reforging. Mammon can assist you."

I reached over my shoulder for my backpack, appraising the demon. For a third time, Mammon laughed, the coif of its hair unmoving as it tilted its head, the single ruby stud in its ear sparkling in the hall's firelight.

"Do not appear so perplexed. Mammon knows the greed that lives in the hearts of men." Another snap, and a large golden bowl appeared on the table. "Set its broken pieces within. Quickly."

Herald nodded encouragingly, and if there was any hesitation left in me, it was long gone. There was something brutally efficient about Mammon's process that should have made me so much more dubious, but I wanted this to end soon. I wanted Vanitas back, the inside of my chest thrumming with that same desire. Want. Need. Now.

Fragments of bronze and shattered garnets tinkled as I spilled the contents of both the wooden chest and my backpack into the bowl. The amulet, the same one that the homunculus had stolen from dad's place, fell in last, its chain spilling among the tangle of ruined verdigris. It struck me that there must have been a reason that the creature singled it out of all the pieces in mom's collection. I retrieved it from the bowl, showed it to Mammon, then slipped it in one of my pockets.

"For safekeeping," I said. "Sentimental value and all that."

Mammon shrugged. "It matters not." The demon snapped its fingers again, and a ruby-encrusted goblet appeared in its hand. It locked gazes with me as it sipped, its eyes scintillant, green, laughing. The goblet vanished, and Mammon leaned over to spit into the bowl through wine-stained lips.

The vessel erupted in a tower of flames so massive that Herald and I staggered back. I shielded my eyes with the back of my hand, seeing just enough to find that the flames had transformed into the shape of Mammon's face.

I couldn't tell where all the screaming was coming from. In a dirge song as of a hundred voices, I heard Mammon's strongest of all, chanting over the infernal chorus. Then I glimpsed it, just beyond the demon's head, one of the paintings. Its occupant's face had changed. I whirled to look at the portraits in the hallway. They were all burning. They were all screaming.

All at once, the fires went out. The paintings went back to normal, but Mammon took the bowl, now gone white-hot, and tipped its contents back. Like magma the liquid metal slipped past bloodless lips, into a slender throat that glowed and blazed from within. Then Mammon stood there, motionless, with its eyes closed.

"This wasn't what I had in mind when we talked about forging and smithing," I whispered to Herald. He glared at me, but said nothing.

"It is a special case for a very special weapon indeed, Dustin Graves."

Mammon smiled with uninjured lips, then coughed, louder, and more violently, until blood spurted in crimson droplets over the marble floor. Herald pulled on my jacket when I rushed to help – as if a demon prince would even need my help.

With one final, gurgling splutter, Mammon heaved something bright red and glistening out of its mouth. It clattered to the floor, smeared in blood. Among the streaks and splotches of gore peeked the object's familiar greenish-gold mix of verdigris and bronze.

"Vanitas," I breathed. Sword and scabbard, all

in one piece.

Mammon chuckled, wiping the corner of its mouth with a silk handkerchief. "Few fires can ever burn hot enough to forge star-metal, but few fires are stronger than those of Mammon's hells. A very taxing service has been completed for you, thing of shadows. Resource-heavy, and complex. The prince of greed demands an appropriate payment."

I gazed at the blood-slicked thing that was Vanitas, then back up at Mammon. I knew I was going to regret the very next words to come out of my mouth, but I wanted my friend back.

"Name your price."

With a mouth that held far, far too many teeth, Mammon smiled.

Even Herald, a self-proclaimed demonologist, held his breath when I answered. Simply being in the demon's palace was having a bizarre effect on me, as if the place was suffused in some invisible gas that made me so desperately eager to have my wishes fulfilled. But I couldn't stop myself, and I knew that I'd sealed my fate.

"Excellent," the demon said. "Then Mammon will call on your aid when the time is right. Permit Mammon time to select the perfect quest for this strangest of men, this thing of shadows. When the time comes – should you refuse – that which you most love shall be taken from you."

I stiffened. That could mean anything. Hell, the quest itself could be anything. But too late. I had what I wanted, and so would the demon, in time. A fine mess I'd gotten myself into. Time was when my biggest problem was figuring out my next paycheck. I never for the life of me expected to owe a favor to a demon. Correction: a demon prince.

"Then Mammon considers this matter settled. You may claim your prize."

Flames consumed the length of Vanitas's blade, marking a scorching, black cross in the marble as it burned the demon's blood away. The fires died out, leaving a shining sword on the ground – at least, as shiny as a tarnished old relic can be.

"Good as new," I said, picking Vanitas up, and surprising myself with his weight. It was like handling a kitchen knife. He weighed hardly anything. I cocked my head questioningly in Mammon's direction.

"Mammon has seen fit to improve the device's enchantments. See how it is lighter now, how it cleaves through the air as a falling leaf dances in autumn."

Herald's glasses seemed to flash in the firelight as he turned his sights on the blade. "But this work is incomplete. The garnets in the blade are dull. The sword should be sentient."

I closed my eyes, reaching to that part of my mind where Vanitas's voice lived. Even with the rough, cold metal of his blade under my fingers, I couldn't sense him at all. Fuck. I'd just agreed to a demon's bargain, and all I had to show for it was a paperweight.

"Mammon only promised to put your plaything back together. Mammon never said it would speak or fly again."

"You piece of – "

"Dust," Herald said warningly, holding a hand against my chest.

Mammon cocked its head, the green of its eyes sparkling with young menace. "Oh? The thing of shadows is displeased, and it thinks to display its temper in such boorish ways. Disrespectful, it is, to Mammon."

"You said you would bring his enchantment back," I snarled. "You said you would make him whole again. You knew that's what I meant."

Mammon sighed, turning its eyes up to the ceiling far, far above us. "For centuries the children of man have spun stories about the trickery of the devil, how Mammon's kind is unreliable, full of deceit, evil. It is not demonkind's fault that your brains are so full of worthless offal." When Mammon looked at me again, I froze. There was a different quality to the demon's eyes this time, not the droll amusement we'd seen when we first entered its domicile. It was something like glee.

"Mammon is no liar. The sword's soul may yet return in time. The thing of shadows is brash, and hot-headed, but it may yet be of service to the princes of hell. For the moment, it suffices to state that Mammon has taken offense. You were initially perceived as an asset. Now, you are something of a liability."

"Damn it," Herald muttered under his breath.

"What's happening?" I said, my grip around Vanitas going even tighter.

"It means that Mammon sees fit to charge a second, smaller price for services rendered. Perhaps even consider it punishment. A penalty. A price you will pay now."

Panic sheared through my chest. "Look," I stammered. "We can talk about this. I didn't mean to – "

"Mammon will find you again, thing of shadows." The demon snapped its fingers. "For now, it is off to your next destination."

Herald and I had no time to move. The floor opened up beneath us. Each of the portraits in the grand hallway laughed in Mammon's voice as we fell, flailing and screaming, into a narrow pit of fire.

Chapter 22

But we didn't burn. In fact, as soon as we plunged into the flames, the world spun on its axis, jostling our brains and bodies, only settling when the fires had cleared. We were – well, we were somewhere else.

It wasn't one of the hells that belonged to the seven demon princes – though if Herald's research was accurate, the number was actually far, far larger than seven. No, a demon wouldn't live in a crystalline chamber, with walls reaching up to a sky so pure and blue, a sky swirling with perfect wisps of cloud.

Wait. I knew this place. We were in Amaterasu's domicile.

The goddess clearly hadn't noticed us. She was balancing a laptop across her knees, sitting cross-legged on an immense mountain of throw pillows. Her mouth dangled half open as she browsed her computer, which again was a fascinating reminder of how the earth's entities had caught up with the times. More remarkable, however, was the onesie she was wearing, its hood in the shape of a fox's head.

"Holy crap," Herald muttered. "It's her. Amaterasu. The goddess of the sun."

"It really is," I said. "Check out the kigurumi she's wearing. Dude, I want pajamas like those. They look so comfy."

Amaterasu giggled at something on her laptop, then stopped herself short, as if sensing that something was amiss. Her eyes slowly swiveled in our direction, and she screamed.

"You!"

"Me," I said. I nudged my thumb at Herald. "Also him. I love your pajammers, by the way. So cute."

The goddess threw off her hood and flushed bright red. "How did you get in here? What is the meaning of this?"

"Oh, Radiant Amaterasu," Herald said, his voice uncharacteristically quavering with what I could only guess was meant to be reverence. "These unworthy ones were delivered here by dire, uncontrollable circumstances. We mean no harm or offense by our intrusion."

Amaterasu rose abruptly to her feet. Her computer slipped off her lap and vanished in a puff of smoke.

"State your name and your purpose, sorcerer."

"This one is named Herald Igarashi. I am an archivist and an alchemist for the Lorica."

Amaterasu's eyes narrowed as they fell on me. "And this one is Dustin Graves. The tainted one. The shadow beast."

I raised a hand sheepishly. "Hi. Nice to see you again."

The goddess scowled. She snapped her fingers, summoning a column of fire to swallow her pajamas. They disappeared in a flash, replaced by the massive, structured raiment I'd once seen her wear, a garment that was equal parts kimono and ceremonial armor. I swallowed thickly. I knew that she could move lightning-quick despite her armor's bulk.

"That's a waste of pajamas," I said.

"I can always order more." Amaterasu sniffed, staring down the end of her nose at Herald. "You. Why have you seen fit to consort with – with that thing?" She folded her arms and raised her head. "Did you say your name was Igarashi? Then we share common roots. Where do your loyalties lie?"

"I," Herald started. "Um."

I put up my hands in placation. "Whoa. Hey. It's the twenty-first century. So not progressive. It's not about that."

"You don't get to talk about progress, shadow beast. As much as your master vouched for you,

you've inevitably proven yourself a force for destruction. An agent for chaos."

Ah. Yes. That old story. The last I'd seen of Amaterasu, I'd visited with Carver. Having him around as a supernatural social buffer meant that she was at least a little more restrained about wanting to chop my head off. There was also this unfortunate incident, that time when I'd accidentally shattered one of her enchanted mirrors. Shush. It was totally accidental. It slipped out of my fingers, and Bastion broke it. You were there, you saw.

"Look," I said. "Is this about the mirror? Because I'm sorry that happened. Even though it technically wasn't my fault."

Herald cleared his throat noisily. "Um. Dust."

"Am I wrong, though? The mirror slipped from my grasp. Bastion was the one who smashed it." I rubbed the back of my neck, giving Amaterasu a piteous look. She wasn't having it.

"The point here," she said slowly, "is that you destroyed something of mine. Something that was freely given for you to use for the sake of good."

"But you can always make more, right?"

My teeth clamped down on my tongue just as soon as I'd said the words. Herald groaned. Carver could teach me to make fire, to nuke planets and move the stars, but fuck if he could teach me any kind of impulse control.

"You enter my domicile unbidden, uninvited,

and think to insult me." The room was getting warmer by the second. The same could be said of Amaterasu's sword, which glowed white-hot, then burst into flames.

"Good job, Dust," Herald muttered. I shrugged apologetically, an empty, pointless gesture, sure, but I had a feeling Amaterasu would take my tongue if I dared to talk again.

"And worse still," Amaterasu continued, "is that you've come to my home carrying your tainted blade."

Vanitas. Oh shit. I lifted him up, along with my other hand, gesticulating wildly. "This? It's nothing. Just bronze."

"You dare to bring the pollution of the Old Ones with you into my home once more." She lifted her head back, sniffed at the air, then scoffed with some measure of triumph. "I smell the stink of demons about you, too." Amaterasu raised her sword, pointing at my heart. "I am not known for brutality and savagery, but for all your breaches of etiquette, you must be punished."

The sole of Herald's boot clacked across the floor as he stepped forward, making himself a human barrier between me and Amaterasu's extremely pointy and extremely fiery sword.

"Offense was not meant, oh Radiant One. Please understand," he said, flinging his hand in my direction, pointing in my face, "this one is unworthy, unlearned in the graces of divinity."

"Hey," I said, somehow finding the gall to be

offended.

"You shut up," Herald growled through gritted teeth. "Let me handle this and shut the fuck up."

But before Herald could speak again, the crisp blue sky over the crystalline walls of Amaterasu's chamber split with a blinding white flash. A tower of lightning speared the ground just feet away from the goddess's dais, leaving in its place not a scorch mark, but a young man.

His hair was swept up into ostentatious waves and spikes, like the electricity had done most of the styling for him. He wore ripped jeans and snazzy sneakers, and went bare-chested under his leather vest. The man could have easily passed Sterling's very specific and very impractical guidelines for fashion, but something told me that he wasn't a vampire. I mean, obviously. We were in a sun goddess's realm, after all.

Light glinted off the man's sunglasses. When he grinned, even his teeth seemed to sparkle, the very paragon of youthful arrogance that Bastion could only hope to be. He took his shades off, pushing them into his hair, and his eyes crackled with little sparks of electricity.

"Sorry I'm late, sis," he drawled.

"Brother," Amaterasu said, her gaze still unflinchingly settled on my face. "Good of you to join us."

"Shit," Herald whispered. "Shit shit shit."

Shit was right. This guy was the reason

Amaterasu hid in a cave in that one ancient story out of myth.

The man raised an eyebrow as he cast an appraising glance over us. "I didn't think you were expecting guests."

Amaterasu's eyes narrowed. "I wasn't expecting them either. Perhaps you'll join me in welcoming them."

The man grinned even wider, his teeth bright with the glimmering of tiny arcs of lightning. He rolled his shoulders, his muscles rippling, joints popping as he did. Uh-oh.

"I wouldn't mind it," he said. "I thought we were just going to binge-watch some shows but this is great, too. I haven't gotten in enough cardio for the week yet."

"This has all been a misunderstanding," Herald said, his voice unnaturally still as he held his hands up in some vain attempt to appease the two gods.

"Aww, come on," the man said. "Stay a while, spar with us. Besides." His eyes flitted to me briefly, and he let off a string of words in Japanese.

"Seriously," Herald said under his breath. "It's the twenty-first century, knock it off."

The man shrugged. "I suppose. Times do change, and I get that. But some of the old ways remain. For example: I haven't changed my weapon of choice."

He reached out his hand, clenching his fingers

around a second lightning bolt that crashed from out of the clear sky. A sizzle, a flash, and the electricity cleared, and suddenly he was holding a sword, crackling with lightning.

Ah. Well. Fuck.

Chapter 23

That sealed it then. The lean, literally electrifying man before us was none other than Susanoo-no-Mikoto, the Japanese god of sea and storm, and brother to Amaterasu.

They'd had their differences in the past, and while mythological stories told that they'd reconciled, I never realized that it meant they were buddy-buddy enough to hang out on weekends to watch movies and eat microwave popcorn. And me, and Vanitas, and Herald? We were in the way of all that.

"This should be fun," Susanoo said.

And no sooner than the last word had left his lips, the god disappeared in a flash of lightning. Amaterasu's eyes gave him away as they darted to a point behind my head. I ducked, and the air occupying the space where my head was brief seconds ago whizzed with the singing of Susanoo's lightning blade.

"Guys, seriously," I yelled, tumbling away and giving myself room to breathe, and hopefully, maneuver. I unsheathed Vanitas, his metal singing as blade and scabbard came apart. "We'll just leave and you can carry on doing whatever it is god-siblings do on weekends. No need to – whoa."

I ducked again as a bolt of fire in the shape of a bird whistled directly at my face, loosed from a single sweep of Amaterasu's sword. She grinned to herself smugly, winding her blade back, and that was all the warning I needed. She slashed, and a dozen fire-birds came screeching out of thin air. I scrambled and dove for the ground just as the flames exploded against the wall behind me.

"Wow, seriously," I said. "We can talk this out."

"Talking is nice," Susanoo said, his voice calm, but his eyes gleaming with boyish delight. "But this? This is fun."

Amaterasu's form wavered, and she vanished from her dais, reappearing just in front of me. I brought Vanitas up to meet her sword, the clash of metal singing through the chamber. If Mammon hadn't reforged him to be lighter, I might have been toast. You know, literally.

She bared her teeth at me, her breath so hot it

may as well have been air from a furnace. "Defeat us and you leave with your lives, shadow beast."

"Heads up," Herald yelled.

The ground around us erupted in a field of icicles, stalagmites instantly manifesting and thrusting upwards like so many frozen spears. Amaterasu shouted as razor-sharp ice tore through the folds of her sleeves, but she struggled free.

I fell into my own shadow as an icicle narrowly missed spiking my entire face, and I tried to use what little time I had in the Dark Room to catch my breath, emerging in the crystal chamber at Herald's side.

"Thanks for the warning," I grumbled.

"Don't get snippy. They're right. The only way out of this is to win. You've done that before, but Amaterasu isn't going to fall for the same tricks twice. You better hope you've got something else up your sleeve, Graves."

I shook my head, as if shaking my own fears and doubts loose. "Hey, we'll handle this. You just gotta trust me. You just gotta trust in – "

I didn't get to finish. The whistling of the air above us was our only warning as Susanoo came crashing out of the sky in a murderous swan dive. I shadowstepped away again, and Herald stumbled as the god's crackling sword cratered the marble floor. Herald rolled to the ground, clutching at his ankle.

In a flash, Susanoo attacked again, bringing

his sword in a sideward slash against Herald's head. Herald raised his hands, a shield made out of solid ice sprouting between his fingers, only just blocking the blow. But Susanoo hacked again, each of his strikes taking great chunks of ice out of Herald's makeshift barrier.

"Dust," he yelled. "Little help."

My heart thumped. This would be so much easier if I could just take a person with me into the Dark Room, but I couldn't pull that off with a homunculus, and even then I'd meant to do it in an attempt to kill. Who knew what the living shadows of the Dark would do to a friend?

But what if that friend wasn't human? What if –

"Better hope this works," I muttered, turning Vanitas in one hand, cutting the smallest nick I could manage in the palm of the other.

The Dark Room wanted its price, so I had to make it count. I knew it would take my blood, but instinct and experience told me that the shadows were stronger, more vicious and volatile each time I willingly gave more of myself. I opened the door, just the fraction of an inch, and a blade of pure darkness erupted from the shadow at Susanoo's feet –

And struck at thin air. He'd disappeared in a flash of electricity, leaving nothing behind but sparks and the smell of ozone. He reappeared again, looking over his shoulder just long enough to grin at me.

"Try again," he said, winking.

"Give up, shadow beast," Amaterasu said, swinging her sword back to prepare another salvo of fire-birds. "We know of your foul tricks."

Not all of them, I thought to myself.

The last of the ice clinked to the ground as Susanoo smashed away all that was left of Herald's shield. Violet light flickered and faded from around Herald's hands. He was out of arcane energy, and with a busted ankle, it wasn't like he had anywhere to go.

"The coup de grace," Susanoo said, his chest puffing out as he gloated. "I want to end this in a most spectacular way."

He threw his sword into the sky, and I watched as it vanished into the clouds, joining a burbling, newly-risen storm that swirled threateningly far above us.

I had to time it right. "Susanoo," I called out. "I'm trying again."

He turned to me, his eyes now as dark as the gathering storm, his laughter as booming and deep as a hurricane. "Go on," he said.

My palm bled freely as I summoned another spear of darkness from the ground, and Susanoo's laughter rang around the crystal chamber as he blinked out of existence once more. There it was – my window of opportunity. I raised Vanitas and hurled him into my own shadow, and he vanished into the Dark Room. Susanoo reappeared, shrugging and grinning smugly, and as he came into existence, so did his shadow.

"Time for your friend to die," Susanoo said. "Sayonara, little sorcerers." A bolt of lightning came crackling down to meet us.

Vanitas zoomed from out of the god's shadow, driven with the same velocity I'd used to throw him. The sword speared the god at an angle, skewering him from spine to sternum.

"Oh," he said, glancing down at the point of the sword sticking out of his chest. The lightning he'd called from the sky no longer seemed interested in Herald, and went rocketing in search of the closest source of metal.

I wasn't expecting that part. How the god screamed.

I'd assumed that Susanoo would have some kind of resistance to lightning, given his portfolio, but maybe electricity really, really hurts when it's conducted by a sword that's stuck through your entire body. I looked away as the smell of burnt flesh filled my nostrils. Between the burbles of pain and the agonized howling, I swore I could hear Susanoo laughing.

"Well played," he gurgled. He hit the ground with a wet thump.

"Brother!" Amaterasu's sword fell from her hand as she rushed to his side, clanging to the floor. I wasn't going to take any chances. If this was our ticket out, then we needed to take our shot.

"Herald. Now."

He slammed his palm into the ground, sharpened pillars of ice rising from around Amaterasu's body, slicing into her robes, pinning her in place. I groaned as I opened slits and slivers of the Dark Room, throwing out a dozen black blades of shadow, sharp enough to stop her in her tracks, to threaten her throat and her heart, but not quite long enough to pierce her skin. Not just yet. We'd trapped her in a cocoon, an iron maiden made out of frost and shadow.

Amaterasu held perfectly still. Her eyes burned through my skull as she glared at me. "You win, shadow beast. Leave now, and let me tend to my brother."

"Show us the exit," I said, "and we're out of here, like, yesterday."

Her lips pursed tight, but a panel slid open in one of the crystal walls around us.

"Go," she commanded coldly.

Focusing on the Dark Room, I closed each of the gaps I'd opened in reality. The shadow blades ensnaring Amaterasu's body vanished. I walked over to Susanoo's twitching form, retrieving Vanitas from his scorched body. He yowled as I yanked the sword out of him. He coughed, then laughed again.

"Defeated by mortals. What a day. I look forward to fighting you again, shadow beast."

"Not any time soon I hope," I said, still averting my eyes. "No hard feelings, okay? Cool.

Bye."

Susanoo said nothing more, only gurgling and chuckling wetly into the ground.

I slid my shoulder under Herald's arm, helping him to his feet. My hand – the bloody one – happened to land on the back of his neck.

"Dust. Aww. Gross."

"Quit your bitching. I'm trying my best."

We hobbled through the exit as Amaterasu blasted the last of the ice imprisoning her, then dashed to her brother's side, kneeling on the marble. Her crystalline chamber dropped like a curtain around us, and from the warmth of her domicile, we were thrust back into the cool, crisp calm of a dewy Valero morning.

I looked around, heaving, and still wincing from the gash in my hand. "Huh. We're where Amaterasu's tether should be. Mrs. Yoshida's garden."

A lovely little zen garden, really, in the backyard of an even littler old lady's house, out in a nicer part of Valero.

Herald slumped to the ground, rearranging his legs against the stone-lined earth, gritting his teeth as he channeled the dregs of his power into his busted foot. The violet light around his fingers flickered, but he sighed in relief all the same. The healing magic must have worked.

"Throw me some of that when you're done, would you?" I watched him a little jealously, the chill air of the morning at least doing its work of numbing the stinging in my hand. "Man. You think Susanoo's going to be okay? I didn't murder him or anything, did I? He wasn't in his domicile, after all."

Herald shook his head. "I don't think so. Susanoo is brash and arrogant, but he wouldn't risk his life. Not for a sparring session. Amaterasu, Susanoo, and the god of the moon are all siblings. They must share power between their domiciles in some way. He wouldn't have just hopped over to hang out at her place if he knew it would make him so vulnerable."

"Oh. Oh good. I don't need more gods on my ass." I wiped at my forehead, the sweat beaded there already cooling like little droplets of ice. "Can you believe? The only entity we've met that didn't want to kill me was a demon."

Herald scoffed. "Dust. Mammon threw us into Amaterasu's dimension, fully knowing that she still held a grudge against you. That was the second price. That was your punishment."

Understanding dawned, and I clenched my hand, then yelped softly, because it was the one with a wound in it. "Damn it, you're right. Something about Mammon's domicile was messing with my head." I was impulsive, even more than usual, and borderline irrational about getting what I wanted.

"Prince of greed," Herald said, shrugging. "Not entirely your fault."

"So demons don't play fair, either." I sighed,

my breath gusting into fog. "Par for the course. I guess I'm not as charming as I thought."

"Well," Herald grunted, pushing himself to his feet. "Muster it up, anyway. We're going to need a little charisma in a minute."

"Huh? What do you – "

Herald's body folded into a bow. "Ohayou gozaimasu, Yoshida-san. Great morning, isn't it?"

The wizened little woman named Mrs. Yoshida looked at each of us, perhaps deciding that she'd had enough of weirdoes turning up in her garden at dawn.

"Ohayou gozaimasu," she said in polite response, before lifting a whistle to her lips and blowing. The whistle made no sound, but the dobermans snarling and racing out from the other side of the house sure did.

Bloodied and broken, we hoofed it out of Mrs. Yoshida's garden, with a small fleet of angry, frothing dogs in hot pursuit. Ah. Nothing like a little bit of cardio at the ass-crack of dawn.

Chapter 24

Eight hours wasn't enough sleep for me to recover. Hell, twenty-four probably wouldn't have made any difference, either, but Sterling was already itching to drag me out again. Literally. I woke up, and he was actually hauling me out of bed and towards the bathroom.

"Get your ass ready, Graves," he said, throwing a towel in my face. "We have an appointment to keep."

Right. The meeting with Diaz. I'd totally forgotten. I groaned, slinging the towel over my shoulders. "Five more minutes?" I bargained.

"We can't miss this," Sterling said. "Because then our only option is to try again tomorrow after nightfall, which is dumb, because what if those homunculi show up again?"

"Fine," I grumbled, scratching at my scalp, smacking my lips. "Wait. How'd you get into my bedroom?"

"I picked the locks. Obviously."

Well. That woke me up. "So you mean you can break in and suck my blood any old time you want now?"

He held a hand to his chest, feigning offense. "Why, I would never do that to you, Dustin. We're friends, aren't we?"

I glowered, and all he did was give me a sly grin.

"Five minutes," he said, "then we leave for Nirvana."

"Huh?"

"Diaz's home," Asher said, ambling into the room. "It's what they call the place where he and his vampire friends live. Remember?"

I raised my eyebrow, looking between the two of them. "Yeah. Is this a wise arrangement?" I lifted a hand, counting off on my fingers. "So that makes one vampire and two human mages. And we're going to a meeting that involves a blood witch and – did you say twelve vampires?"

"Diaz specifically asked for Asher to come along." Sterling shrugged. "Besides. I can take 'em. Push comes to shove, I handle twelve of them, and you take the human."

"Be serious."

"It's nothing to worry about," Asher said. "Carver gave me this. In case of emergency, he said." Beaming, he raised something on a chain around his neck, holding it out in front of his face. It was a pendant, set with an amber gem. Huh.

"Fine," I said. "Okay. That makes me feel a little better."

Sterling tugged on Asher's shirt to get a closer look, clapping him on the shoulder and mumbling small assurances about his safety. Asher didn't seem to care, if I'm honest. He looked positively thrilled to be walking into a den of lions.

We took a rideshare out from the front of Mama Rosa's restaurant. Sterling pouted and muttered over how we totally should have booked something as luxurious as Bastion's ride. Asher was just happy to be there, happy to be out in the world.

He clung to his window, face pressed up against the glass, curious about every damn thing he saw. It was hard to hate him for it. He sat there staring, even seeming to appreciate the increasingly crappy urban landscape as our car crossed from the Meathook over into the Gridiron.

We got out on the sidewalk somewhere in the industrial district, not very far from where Sterling and I had encountered Other-Dustin. Somewhere in the night, I could hear the furious pump of angry house music. Industrial house music, even. Hah, I'm such a genius. Our driver, a friendly Eastern European dude with a thick accent and an even thicker beard, told us to watch our backs.

"Is not safe," he said.

Asher waved amicably as the man drove off. Sterling scoffed.

"Not safe for the locals, maybe." He thumbed his chest. "Get it? 'Cause we're here now?"

"Right," I said. "Very funny. Asher, did Carver explain your contingency plan at all? Do you know what your amulet does?"

Fire a beam of concentrated sunlight, I was hoping he would say. Cast a single-use batch of protective shells around each of the three of us in case things got hairy.

"Oh." He lifted his hand to his throat, his pendant glinting in the streetlight. "He says I just have to break this." He tapped the gem lightly with his fingernail. "Then it'll teleport me back to the Boneyard."

"Just you?"

Asher nodded.

I looked up into the sky, hoping Carver could hear me. "Damn it to hell, Carver."

"Relax," Sterling said. "Don't be such a baby. It's just like you to worry about this shit. Look at Asher. He's fine."

Asher beamed.

"Listen. You've been in tighter spots. You commune with gods who poison you and want to rip your head off, like, all the time. This is going to be a cakewalk."

I squinted at him. "You're being awfully nice to me for some reason."

Sterling shrugged, wearing his most winning smile. His fangs glinted. "Hey. I'm a swell guy." He cracked his knuckles. "Also, if anyone asks, it's way less complicated if we just pretend you're both my thralls."

He said that in one breath, and way too quickly, like he didn't want me hearing. "Whoa, wait, what?"

"Awesome," Asher said. "I'm a thrall."

Kid's sweet. I never said he was very smart.

"Just shut up and follow my lead."

Sterling rolled his shoulders, his leather jacket squeaking as he did, and he smoothed back his hair. Suddenly he seemed taller, and maybe a bit stronger. Asher and I followed as Sterling led the way to a short flight of steps, down to a door that was hidden just below street level.

"Password," said a voice on the other side.

"Your mom's chest hair," Sterling said. He pounded on the door with one fist, though not nearly strong enough to break it down the way I knew he could. This was his idea of being polite.

"Sterling?" the voice said. "Is that you? Come on, you know the rules. I'll get in trouble if you don't say it." The voice was trying its hardest to be authoritative, but mainly just came off sounding pitiful.

Sterling rolled his eyes. "What feeds in

darkness grows ever stronger," he droned.

"Awesome," the voice said. The door cracked open, revealing an exceedingly tall and exceedingly pimply youth, dressed in what must have been his idea of vampiric attire. He was fair-skinned, but not quite pale enough to be one of the undead. "Thanks for playing," he said, ushering us in.

We stepped through and continued to a bare cement corridor, the ceiling lined with industrial piping, the walls lined with a whole lot of nothing. That distant music kept playing, though, and I imagined it coming from the secret underground sex dungeon-cum-dance club that I'd seen in, like, basically every movie about vampires, ever. I chuckled to myself.

"So that guy," Asher said. "I'm guessing he wasn't a vampire."

"Rudy? Nah. Just a hanger-on. Keeps hoping he'll get turned some day, but that's up to the vampires in Diaz's coven to decide."

I raised an eyebrow, walking faster to keep up with Sterling. "Whoa, whoa. A coven? Is that what you call a gang of vampires?"

"We call ourselves what we like. A clan, a pack, a murder of vampires. Does it really matter? The distinction is that Diaz is a blood witch. It's why he refers to his family as a coven."

"Family, huh?"

Sterling stopped at what seemed like a random point in the hallway, turning to me with half a grin on his lips. "When everyone you know and everyone you love is dead and gone, you don't have much of a choice. You pick and gather your allies, your friends. It's both a perk and a curse, but when you're undead – you get to choose your family."

"Am I part of your family?" Asher asked, all unabashed innocence. He took the words right out of my mouth.

Sterling smiled, ruffling Asher's hair. "If you want. Sure you are, little buddy."

Huh. So we were his family? The Boneyard. Carver, Gil, Mama Rosa, even me. Asher chuckled, running his hands through his hair in an attempt to fix it. Sterling turned towards the wall, then rapped his knuckles against the cement. It made a hollow knocking sound.

"Ah. Some things don't change." He rested his hand against the wall, and it slid open.

The room beyond was barer than I expected, like the inside of a warehouse, only underground. It looked like a bunker, or an industrial basement. Cement walls, cement floor, cement ceiling, but done up in luxuries that I could only describe as plush.

Nirvana had thick rugs, comfy sofas, and even several tastefully placed potted plants. I admit, I was sorely wrong about the S&M dungeon I was expecting. The only real indication that vampires inhabited this place was the decorator's overwhelming proclivity towards the color red.

Well, that, and all the coffins. At least the ones that I could see. The absence of windows meant that the vamps living in Nirvana – or unliving, rather – didn't really need closed caskets to sleep in, but I guess old habits die hard. I didn't realize that Sterling's preference for sleeping in an actual bed, you know, the kind meant for human beings, made him more modern and progressive than his brethren.

All of whom were stunningly beautiful. You could tell they were human, once, if only in shape and name, but I was caught like a deer in headlights. Asher was similarly enthralled. Everything about these creatures was heightened, from the sharpness of their eyes and their cheekbones to the perfection of their bodies. Skin, whether black or brown or white, was supple, flawless, lustrous. Turns out that becoming one of the undead was better than any moisturizer.

The vampires milled about, chatting, laughing. A couple were playing video games. One sat in a corner, reading. Among them were humans. Thralls, I assumed, but no one was chained, put on a leash, none of the stereotypes I would have expected from mortals who would serve as human cattle for their vampire companions. There was something, I don't know, consensual about it all. I guess Sterling was right all along. I did have some prejudices about vampires.

I spotted Connor, the big, bald vampire who'd

attacked me in the alley, towards the back of the room, working on weights that no one should be capable of lifting. Salimah turned her head towards us as we entered, balancing a glass of something that could have been blood, or could have been a very rich wine in one hand. She nodded at us, then towards the center of the vast underground apartment.

Sitting there like the still, unmoving eye of Nirvana's storm was Diaz, a lean, swarthy young man in a loose tank top and fitted jeans. As he approached us, I noted that he was barefoot – vulnerable, yet comfortable in what I could still only perceive as a den of apex predators.

"Sterling," Diaz said, his smile warm and welcoming. "It's been a while."

"Diaz. These are my – companions." He gestured at us. "This is Dustin, and this is Asher."

Diaz's smile went even wider, his eyes crinkling. "Ah. The shadow mage. And this one must be the necromancer. Younger than I expected."

"Can't help it," Asher said, shrugging and offering a smile of his own.

Diaz chuckled. "Come. We have things to discuss."

He led us towards the back of the room, to a table close to where Connor was still bench pressing what must have been the equivalent weight of a loaded refrigerator. His eyes flitted nervously between me and Sterling. I smiled, but he only gave a grunt. Or maybe that was just from the strain of lifting. Who knows, really.

Diaz gestured at the shrouded object spread out on the table. I skidded to a halt when I realized that it wasn't just a bunch of stuff with a cloth thrown over it. There was a body underneath.

I was aware that the room was still humming with activity, but there was a different quality to the bustle now. The vampires were going about their business more reservedly, as if they were straining to listen.

"Now," Diaz said, folding his hands. "Dustin, was it? I must apologize for my colleagues' earlier behavior. My undead companions are very protective of me, you see. That sense of responsibility extends to my collection of curiosities, the Heartstopper among them." He clapped me on the shoulder, squeezing with a firm touch. "Let me be the first to apologize for how crudely Connor treated you."

I heard one or two restrained snorts go around the room. The vampires were keeping tabs on us after all. Connor grunted even louder, and this time he set his weights down on the ground, as if to pay us his fullest attention. The earth moved the tiniest bit as his barbell clanged to the floor.

"You know, don't worry about it. No harm done. I gotta admit, I admire how you guys can interact so harmoniously." I chuckled and nudged a thumb over at Sterling. "I can barely get along with this one. It's a work in progress."

Sterling hissed. I shrugged. Diaz chuckled.

"I confess, my abilities play some part in that. The dynamic I maintain with my twelve undead companions is wonderfully symbiotic. They offer protection, strength, and – entertainment."

He turned his head so subtly when he spoke, as if to display the series of scars on his neck, around his clavicles, on his shoulders, little raised dots where fangs had punctured his skin. I tried not to swallow.

"In return I offer magical support, the many gifts brought by my artifacts, and to an extent, wisdom." He held his hand out to Sterling. "You said you had a sample for me to examine."

Sterling riffled through his pockets, then extracted one of the phials of blood that he had taken from the homunculus at the warehouse.

"How the hell did you manage to keep that fresh?" I asked. "You have a fridge in your bedroom?" I blinked, then turned to Asher. "Dude, do you have a personal fridge, too? Am I the only one who – "

"Shut up," Sterling said. "The phial's special. It's from Diaz."

"The vampires of Valero come to me with their needs." Diaz took the phial, holding it up and examining it in the light, then letting it roll around in the palm of his hand. "These phials hold a very minor enchantment that helps preserve the organic matter contained within.

The same enchantment that allows the Heartstopper to preserve dead flesh."

He uncorked the stopper, then tipped a couple of drops of blood directly onto his tongue. Around us, the vampires were transfixed, their eyes glued to the phial in the blood witch's hand. Diaz smacked his lips once, twice, savoring the blood.

"Sterling was right. This is horrible. Inorganic, and thin. Very much the same quality of blood as we found on this corpse."

Ah. So it was a corpse after all. I held my breath, even though I fully knew what to expect when Diaz threw the sheet off the body. Spread over the table was a perfect copy of Dustin Graves, pale in death, stark naked, with a teardrop-shaped ruby in the hollow of its chest. Sterling gave the corpse a once-over, then made a low whistle.

"Not bad, Graves."

Asher murmured his assent.

"Sterling. Stop perving over my dead body. And Asher, just – you two need to shut up."

"On the contrary," Diaz said, "we'd very much like for Asher to use his communicative talents. This creature stole my Heartstopper, one of my own signature enchantments, then returned within a matter of days, doubtless with the intent to steal another one of my artifacts. But we were ready for him this time."

I didn't ask how the homunculus died, but the

puncture marks on its neck and chest should have been a clue.

"I'm amazed you managed to preserve it this way," I muttered, reaching out to press on the thing's forearm. It was cold, and stiff to the touch. I tried not to think about how I would look very much the same if I was dead. This was how I must have looked the night Thea sacrificed me, splayed naked across an altar.

"It's the Heartstopper's doing. The artificial quality of the homunculus's blood was a clue that something was not quite right. Its form lacks a firmament, something fundamental to bind its body together."

Asher piped in. "You mean a soul?"

"Exactly. Without it, Dustin's clones can barely hold the threads of their sordid lives together. That they can exist at all suggests that there is a glimmer of something that keeps them alive. Asher. I'd like for you to commune with this creature's spirit – or whatever vestiges that could be considered its spirit."

"Oh, wow. Yeah. I could certainly try."

"And then maybe it can show us where to find the others," I said. "Stem the tide at its source." Find Thea, and kill her.

"Yes," Diaz said. "Precisely what I had in mind."

He stepped aside, beckoning Asher to approach. Sterling nudged him encouragingly, pushing between his shoulder blades. Asher took his place at the end of the table just above the homunculus's head. He laid a hand on each of the corpse's temples, then shut his eyes. Everyone in the room – mortal or vampire – fell into complete silence.

It didn't take long for his talent to manifest itself. Through his lessons with Carver, Asher had further refined his ability to communicate with the dead. It was part of his portfolio, after all, this historically sought-after talent to exert power over death itself. That rarest of gifts made Asher a valuable asset to the Boneyard, and someone I was glad to have on my side.

Green tendrils of energy curled like snakes from Asher's elbows down to the creature's head, wrapping and writhing until they slithered into every exposed orifice. I fought the bile rising in my throat as filaments of emerald power wriggled their way into the corpse's eye sockets, its nostrils, its ears. I watched, waiting for the thing to speak through Asher, or perhaps for Asher to hear its voice in his head and convey its message to us.

I didn't expect for Other-Dustin's dead eyes to flicker open and stare directly at me, for it to speak in my own voice.

Chapter 25

The homunculus smiled at me. There was none of the characteristic malice I'd come to expect from its breed, just an odd expression I could only describe as serenity. I'd go as far as to say familiarity.

"Brother," it whispered.

My blood froze. This thing wasn't my brother, not by any means, whether natural or paranormal. When the creature said it again, I wondered why my heart twinged with an emotion I couldn't name.

"We need answers," Diaz said, with all the gentleness of a doting parent.

Something in his demeanor went even looser, and as calming as his presence was before, it made him radiate even more of his unusual charisma, perhaps the same kind of magnetism that allowed him to pacify and even befriend an entire brood of the bloodthirsty undead.

The homunculus brought its black eyes to gaze at Diaz with something approaching fondness. It blinked slowly, and nodded. Asher kept his hands on the creature's temples, maintaining a steady flow of necromantic force to keep the channel open.

Diaz's voice was whisper-soft. "How many of you are there?"

"Many," my voice answered. "Very many."

Somehow, that felt more chilling than any concrete number the creature could have given us.

"I don't think it's lying," I said quietly. "They have very basic intelligence. They can only really parrot information. But many could mean anything."

"Many could mean anything," the homunculus echoed, smiling at me with my own lips, the wrinkle beside its left eye crinkling the way it would on my own face.

"Your brothers," Diaz continued. "Are they like you? Are they stronger, or do they hold the same power?"

"Same," it said lazily, blinking again, its eyes caught in an odd kind of distant reverie. "All the same. All brothers."

"Then we know that they have the same level of strength. The same talents." Sterling gave a slow, relieved sigh. "At least we know they aren't all like you, Dust. Imagine an army of these things that could use shadow and fire."

Dread twisted in my stomach, as if anything about this doppelganger situation could possibly be any worse. For a fleeting moment I saw copies of myself roaming Valero, flinging fire and conjuring blades of night to slaughter and kill.

"Yeah," I said evenly. "Good thing."

"Guys," Asher said, sweat glazing his forehead. "I can't hold the connection much longer. Its life essence is slipping. Last questions, now."

"Very well." Diaz stepped closer to the table, bending to look into the homunculus's eyes. "Where are your brothers?"

"A field. With grass. And stones. Big, flat stones, and bones below. Buried bones."

"A graveyard," Sterling said. "It's describing a graveyard."

"Latham's Cross?" I folded my arms, staring at the ground as if it could give me the answers I needed. "That's the biggest graveyard in Valero. Their base couldn't be that far out of the city, or the attacks wouldn't have come so frequently."

"Sounds about right," Sterling said.

"Guys," Asher grunted. "Last question. The body'll break down any moment."

He got that right. The homunculus began to twitch, its face twisting with what first looked like discomfort, then pain. Diaz placed his hand on its forehead. For a moment, the homunculus stilled and settled.

"Dying?" the creature said, in a plaintive voice that wrenched at my chest. Why was I feeling for this creature? All we shared was our blood. I owed it nothing, not even sympathy.

"I'm sorry." Diaz nodded, his eyes lowered, his mouth drawn. "Before you go. Who made you?"

"White Mother," it answered, its eyes glazed with a mix of fright and reverence. "White Mother tells us where to go. What to take." It blinked again, its eyes flitting about the room, the ceiling, as if searching for something. "White Mother sends us again and again. She sends so many brothers tonight."

Many brothers? Tonight?

"Where are they now?" Diaz asked, his voice so soft that I nearly missed how it was trembling.

The homunculus writhed and twitched on the table, as if wracked by some hideous agony. It was in the throes of death. Its head slammed against the table as its neck bent back. Then, like a rubber band released, the tension left the thing's body, and it collapsed against the table again, soft, loose, languid. It smiled, then it whispered.

"They're here."

Diaz stepped back, his face a mask of shock, and Asher yelled as he tore his hands away, the necromantic energy receding into his fingers. The homunculus screamed as its body dissolved into goo, its skin and meat and bones sloughing and dripping to the ground. I watched as the Heartstopper rolled off the table and clattered into a puddle of gore.

Then the door burst open. Heads spun as we turned to face our attackers. My heart pounded like war drums, and the tension caught in my throat.

First five, then ten, then at least two dozen men who looked just like me poured into the room, each wearing the same gleeful leer, each mouth locked in an expression of demonic ferocity. They tore through Nirvana, savaging the human thralls, breaking bones and faces with makeshift clubs, planks of wood, lengths of pipe. The homunculi fought with inhuman brutality, and with terrifying precision, expertly singling out every mortal in the room, prioritizing their injuries and deaths.

We scattered. The vampires leapt into the fray, tearing into the homunculi with fists and fangs, and springing back when they found that the creatures were equipped with strength that far surpassed human bounds. Diaz shouted as he flung spells across the room, scarlet beams of energy blasting homunculi off their feet.

Sterling, Asher, and I stuck together in our own unit, our backs towards each other for protection. I knew I heard Sterling attempting to strategize, but it was hard to make anything out over the roar and clamor of battle.

More of the homunculi were pouring into the

room with each passing minute, replacing those slain by the might of the coven. I glanced at my palm, then the door, waiting for the right moment to tear my wound open, to pay the blood price I needed to give in exchange for the magnified eldritch power of the Dark Room.

Between studying and waiting for an opening, I somehow picked it out. A single homunculus had stayed out of the thick of battle. Now it strode confidently for the center of the room, something at its throat pulsating like a distant star.

It was a gem. A shining, white opal.

"No," I said, the dreadful realization prickling at my skin. "Diaz. Get your coven out of here. Now."

I could tell he heard from the way his eyes bore into me for the fraction of a second, but he turned back to the battle, forging on in fury. I tugged on Sterling's jacket.

"Sterling, you need to get the fuck out of here."

"I can help," he said. "No way I'm leaving. These are my kind, and – "

"Asher," I shouted. "Your pendant. Use it on him."

Asher clutched Carver's amulet, scanning the room, and found exactly what I saw: the homunculus, its jewel glowing rhythmically, like the timer on a bomb.

"Oh shit," Asher said. He ripped the necklace off his neck, wrenched Sterling by the collar, then smashed the jewel into his forehead. It shattered, issuing a tiny puff of smoke.

Sterling clutched at his brow, his teeth bared. "The fuck are you doing, Mayhew? If you think for a second that – "

Sterling vanished before he could finish his sentence, teleported instantly to the Boneyard through the smashed jewel's enchantment. Asher stepped to my side, clinging to my arm.

"You did the right thing," I said.

"It's happening." He pointed at the homunculus. "Look."

"Diaz," I screamed.

Too late.

The gem at the homunculus's throat shone stronger, brighter, until it flooded the entire room with the force of its brilliance. But this wasn't the smothering light that Thea had once used to blanket the entire city of Valero in a shroud of white. This was something more natural, and more dangerous.

Sunlight.

Twelve voices screamed in dire agony as the raw fury of the sun itself flooded the room, its rays reaching every corner of the underground lair. Those same twelve voices were throttled into grave silence as the blinding light receded. I removed my hand from my eyes. Where the vampires of the coven once stood were only piles of dust. Diaz fell to his knees, his mouth open, his eyes huge with disbelief.

I ran to Diaz's side, pulling Asher with me. "Stay close," I said. "Don't move."

I reached for the shards of broken gemstone in Asher's hand, using their jagged edges to carve a fresh line in my palm. I scanned the room for the thirteen or so homunculi still remaining, marking their places in my mind's eye.

Everywhere but here, I thought, looking at my feet, reaching to the ethers, to the corners of the chamber my soul called home. Bring terror to this world, just, everywhere but here.

Spears of blackest night erupted from the shadows, each skewering a homunculus from spine to skull. Even from where I stood I felt their muscles twitching against my blades, the warmth of corrupted blood running down their razor edges. I felt, too, the tide of warmth running down my palm, the sticky, slick red of my own blood as the Dark Room drank its share of my life force.

I snapped the door shut. The blades vanished, and twelve, thirteen bodies slumped to the floor, lifeless.

"Holy shit," Asher muttered. "You killed them all."

He caught me as I stumbled, my knees stinging as I crumpled to the ground. Through bleary eyes I surveyed the room, the panoply of corpses littering what was once the coven's home, what used to be Nirvana.

But one of the corpses was moving.

We missed one. Scratch that. We missed two. They had feigned death, completely bypassing my assault by blending into the piles of fallen human thralls. The homunculi rushed Diaz, grabbing his arms, one slugging him in the face to stop his words mid-incantation, the other reaching into its shirt to pull out another opal amulet.

Asher broke into a sprint. "No," I shouted, too winded, too exhausted to chase him, or to even summon another blade from the Dark. Diaz and the homunculi vanished in a flash of white light before Asher could even reach them. He skidded to a halt, shielding his eyes against the radiance, cursing under his breath.

"I could have gotten them," he shouted. "I almost got them."

"Don't," I said. "Not your fault. We'll find him."

"How?"

A pillar of flame exploded in the center of the room. I groaned, clenching my wounded hand as I searched my body for any reserves of fight I could muster. Then the flames cleared. It was Sterling, Carver, and Gil.

Gil spun in a circle, his eyes wide. "What the hell happened here?"

"This was a massacre," Sterling said. "I could have helped. I should have stayed." He glared at Asher, his eyes full of accusation.

"You would have died," Carver said, his voice heavy with authority. "Asher did the right thing,

Sterling. Do not fault him for saving your life."

Sterling said nothing, his fist clenched. Asher was quiet, too, but he stuck his hands in his pockets and kicked at the ground.

Gil bent down, sifting through the ashes, sniffing at his fingers. "This is insane. These were all vamps, all killed by sunlight. I can still smell it."

"They were murdered," Sterling growled.

"We have to find them," I said. "They killed every vampire in the coven, then they took Diaz. I don't know what they're going to do with him, but we have to find him."

"Latham's Cross," Sterling said. "That's our best bet."

"Then that's where we'll head." Carver swept his hand across my back, and I felt the warmth of his magic seep into my skin, the flow of blood from my palm slowing, then stopping. "This is the best I can afford for now," he whispered. "We'll need the rest of our energies to fight."

I nodded, staring into his eyes, the words forming in my mouth even though I knew he didn't need to hear them.

"Thea's behind it all," I said. "It's been her all along."

Carver beckoned for us to approach, and we gathered around him in a tight circle.

"Then we're going to find her." He gestured with his hands as he cast a sending spell, trails of amber fire dancing at his fingers as he worked.

"And we're going to kill her."

Chapter 26

Latham's Cross was the closest graveyard for miles around the city. It sat on the outskirts, and based on the homunculus's description, was our only real lead on where to find Thea and the rest of my clones. Drained as I was, I steeled myself, readying body and mind for the inevitable search throughout the graveyard.

We didn't have to look very far.

The sending spell teleported us to the edge of the cemetery. The pillar of eerie white light humming up on a hill gave away Thea's position. There was no point questioning her adherence to the Veil.

She'd abandoned any pretense of hiding the arcane underground from the normals a long time ago, the way she'd forsaken her humanity.

Briefly I wondered whether Latham's Cross had a night caretaker. Knowing Thea, he would have been dead long before we arrived.

The open space, the grass, so many gravestones – it just made the night feel colder. The small dose of healing Carver had granted me was enough to staunch the bleeding, but my palm still felt wet.

I flexed both my hands, testing if I still had the strength left to swordfight with Vanitas. Just in case I had no magic left to give, just in case I needed him. I checked on my backpack, keeping pace with the others as they rushed for the hilltop.

"I'll rip her heart out through her throat," Sterling said. "I'll crush it to a pulp and watch her die."

"Steady," Gil said, clapping Sterling on the back. "Keep your head on straight. You're no good to us if you go wild."

"Says the werewolf," Sterling muttered.

"Enough," Carver said. "There. Do you see?"

We were close enough to be heard, and certainly close enough to be spotted, but the element of surprise wouldn't have helped us anyway. Stealth was pointless. Thea would know we were coming, which explained why she had a horde of homunculi gathered on the hill.

They stood in a large ring, facing outwards, like sentinels, guarding the wavering beam of light in their midst. A white figure moved among them. I couldn't find Diaz, but I couldn't spot an altar, either. I decided that it was at least a good sign.

"Asher, to the rear," Carver said. "Dustin, you follow behind me. Sterling and Gil, to my side."

We formed wordlessly into a loose cross as Carver instructed, a flimsy arrowhead with him at its center. I counted at least forty homunculi from the half of the circle facing us alone. I couldn't make out how densely they populated the hill. For once I wished we had the Lorica for backup.

"Follow my lead," Carver said, stalking up the hill. Twenty, forty pairs of eyes turned to follow us, but the homunculi didn't move from their positions. They might have been waiting for us to approach striking distance. Maybe Thea had given them instructions to stand their ground.

Carver spoke a word that was somewhere between a hiss and a shriek, then flicked his hand in a narrow arc. Pale fire cascaded from his fingers, lancing across the front ranks of the homunculi, filling the night with the horrific crack of breaking bones. Some bent over double, others collapsed to the ground, but none, not one, showed any signs of pain. They only stared at us, every mouth frozen in an awful rictus grin.

"These things are messed up," Gil said.

"You think so? They all have my face. Try that on for size."

I reached over my shoulder, digging into my

backpack's pocket dimension for Vanitas. Maybe it was a reflex. I knew he still couldn't fight on his own – and truthfully I had no guarantee that he ever would again – but having him in my hand made some strange difference. I felt armed. I felt almost prepared.

The homunculi parted, or at least the ones facing us did, creating a gap in their ranks. Slowly, like some demented empress, Thea strode forth, calm, confident, regal.

It was only through the traces of her facial features that I could recognize her. She must have completed the transformation that the Eldest had intended. Plates of gleaming white chitin covered her torso, arms, and legs, like armor. Her eyes were totally black, completely insectoid, reflecting the light from their many facets, like shards of obsidian. And in place of hair her head had grown horned protrusions, twisted into the shape of an ivory crown. Yet if this was what the Eldest had planned for her, then Thea should have considered herself fortunate. I remembered Agatha Black, and I shuddered.

As she approached, I caught a glimpse of what looked like junk, piled into a heap on the hilltop, just at the base of the pillar of light. The light hummed and whistled, giving off a dissonant, alien melody. As we neared the top of the hill I saw what the junk really was: all the trinkets, relics, and magical artifacts that the homunculi had gathered for their White Mother. This was another one of her rituals.

"Come now," Thea said, her voice drifting down the hillside. "Let us not be so violent with each other. I'm sure we can come to some sort of arrangement."

The flatness of her voice, her outright mockery drove a spike through my heart. I gripped Vanitas harder, my hand slipping over his hilt from sweat.

"We haven't come to talk, abomination," Carver said, his voice booming. "We have come to exterminate your filth."

"Ah," Thea said, her eyes glittering with malice. "Then let us speak in your language."

She snapped her fingers. Two of the homunculi emerged, dragging Diaz between them. One punched him in the stomach. Diaz fell to his knees. Thea grasped him by the hair, then settled her talons across his throat.

"Let him go," I shouted. "He has nothing to do with this."

"On the contrary: he has everything to do with this. Come closer, and I kill him."

Gil growled, his claws extending as the flesh of his fingers burst into spurts of gore. Sterling was visibly shaking.

"Enough of this stupidity," Carver snarled. He slashed his arm in a wide arc, and the hillside glowed with a burst of orange light. Every homunculus toppled to the ground, asleep.

Thea was unimpressed. She placed her hands on Diaz's temples, her luminescent talons framing his face. For a moment, he screamed. And then silence. He opened his eyes again. They were totally blank.

Thea raised her head. "Serve your purpose, blood witch."

"Sanguinare," Diaz said, his voice low, and flat.

All across the hillside the homunculi wriggled back to wakefulness, screaming, clawing at their faces as blood ran from their eyes, their ears, their nostrils. By the light of the massive pillar atop the hill I could see the grass run red with their blood. Something terrible was happening here, and I didn't know what.

Thea released Diaz's temples, and his eyes flickered back to brown. They rolled into the back of his head, and he collapsed to the earth. Thea turned in place, surveying the perfect circle of blood she'd inscribed around the hill, and smiled.

"They serve so many purposes, these homunculi. I needed them to retrieve enough magical detritus for my offering, you see. And what better way to cover my tracks than to use your face, Dustin Graves?"

I stared in horror at the corpses littering the grass, knowing that within minutes, all of them would disintegrate into so much worthless gore. "Then why bother creating so many?"

"I needed their blood. Your blood. And the

most efficient way to extract so much of it, all at once, was with a blood witch. Far more practical than butchering them all myself. You've proven yourself a dangerous adversary, Dustin. As a sacrifice, you would have been incredibly useful. The blood of your brothers may be inferior, but in great enough quantities, it still makes a suitable ingredient for a grand communion."

Carver traced patterns with his hands, readying another spell. "You know as well as I that nothing good will come of communing with the Eldest, Thea. They will corrupt you into a useless twist of flesh. Fight us, and you will surely die. Cease your madness now. Surrender."

Thea smiled. "I politely decline your offer." She raised her hand. "Kill them."

From behind her, the pillar's wail grew even louder, a speck of black in its center expanding, until it opened into a rift. A gateway. Tentacles probed the entrance, ebony and slick, savoring the wet air.

"This shit again," Sterling said.

Gil's howl curdled my blood. He'd already gone full dog, speeding up the hillside in his wolf form, a glistening blur of fur and fangs and talons.

The first of the many-tentacled horrors stepped through the gateway, shambling jerkily into our reality. Ah. Of course. I was wondering when the shrikes were going to show up.

Chapter 27

I raised Vanitas, following Carver up the hill. "I wish I had more interesting ways to express just how tired I am of this shit."

Carver led with his hand, clenching his fist and disintegrating three of the shrikes into powder. "I wouldn't take this so casually, Dustin. The homunculi might have been inferior copies of your corporeal form, but arcane blood is arcane blood. Thea has performed powerful ritual magic. We must be on our guard."

"Understood," I said, bracing myself to meet the shrikes. Sterling and Gil had corralled them near the line of blood traced by the homunculi, but more and more of the creatures were streaming out of Thea's portal. I shouted over my shoulder. "Asher. Hang back. Don't get yourself hurt."

"I can help," he said, moving faster, keeping pace.

"Stay out of the way, and stick close to Carver whenever you can."

"But I can help."

I admired his tenacity, but we didn't need anyone else getting hurt tonight. I loosed a battle cry as I charged up the hill, slashing Vanitas in an arc and disabling a shrike, hacking off half of its tentacles in a single blow. Mammon's demonic craftsmanship didn't just make Vanitas lighter. It made him far sharper, too. I tried not to think of what the demon prince had in store for me in exchange for the sword's augmented power.

Neither the time nor the place. I chopped, and hacked, and slashed, wielding Vanitas with renewed confidence. Things were so different on the hill at Latham's Cross than on the night I had first fought the shrikes. One of them had almost killed me then. But not this time. This time was better. I hadn't even used my shadow magic yet and I'd already downed half a dozen.

Something felt off. This was – it was all too easy.

In the midst of the chaos, standing by the pile of magical ornaments, Thea watched us with cold, unfeeling eyes. She almost seemed bored. Unthreatened. I hadn't even seen her launch a single spell. She waved her hand, gesturing at the gateway, and somehow more – impossibly more shrikes poured out of the portal.

This was bad news. I spoke too soon. In the battle at Central Square, there were dozens of mages from the Lorica fighting with us, experienced Hands and even Scions among them. When we last encountered Thea, we had Bastion, Prudence, Romira, and Vanitas to shore up our ranks. All we had tonight was a ragtag bunch of the undead.

Sure, we had a vengeful vampire and a furiously violent werewolf on our side, but we'd be overwhelmed soon enough. For the first time since we showed up I had the feeling that the Boneyard had bitten off more than it could chew. I glanced over at Carver. He was holding off huge numbers of the shrikes on his own, but lich, sorcerer, it didn't matter. A mage was a mage, and we all had limitations to our power.

I fought off another shrike with Vanitas in one hand, then rummaged in my jeans pocket with the other, looking for my phone. I don't know what the hell I was thinking, but maybe getting in touch with the Lorica would help us. Herald, Prudence, Bastion, anybody. Hell, why hadn't anyone shown up? Had Thea cast a glamour over the entire graveyard? Shit. Maybe she did respect the Veil, after all, even if it was for her own perverted purposes.

I retreated, still riffling through my pockets for my cell – where the hell was it? – when I bumped into something. I whirled, brandishing Vanitas in front of me. Good thing I didn't swing him any further – it turned out that I'd bumped into Asher.

"I told you to hang back," I said. "What are you doing?"

"I said I could help, but you wouldn't listen."

He pulled something out of his pocket, then lifted it to the sky. His hand pulsed with the sickly green energy of his necromantic power, and from between his fingers shone the blood-red glow of the Heartstopper.

"What the – where did you – "

"Picked it up at Nirvana," he muttered. "Also: get out of the way."

I obeyed and hauled ass immediately. Asher yelled as he thrust his arm forward, directing the fused forces of his own gift and the Heartstopper's magic in a braided twine of arcane power. My eyes scanned the hillside, waiting for his magic to take effect. It exceeded anything and everything I'd expected.

One by one, the bloodied and broken bodies of the homunculi rose from the earth, balefully resurrected by Asher's necromantic energies. The Heartstopper must have preserved them as he prepared a reanimation spell powerful enough to affect nearly a hundred corpses.

I stood and watched, aghast, as the risen dead joined the fight against the shrikes. The homunculi demonstrated their unholy strength in full force, quite literally tearing the abominations apart, tentacle by tentacle, limb from limb, using nothing but their bare hands.

"Holy shit, Asher."

"Well done," Carver called out from across the way, his eyes sparkling with all of a father's pride. "Brilliantly played, Asher."

Asher grunted as he hefted the stone up high, wielding it like a weapon, a torch. His eyes bulged with terror, shock, and exhilaration, like this was his first true taste of power. I couldn't have been more relieved. The extra bodies he raised meant that we finally had a fighting chance against the shrikes.

"Join the others," Carver said, pointing at Sterling and Gil. "Asher and I will stay back. We need him to maintain the reanimation spell as long as he can. I'll protect him."

"Copy," I said, rushing into the gap that vampire and werewolf had so surgically hacked among the shrikes.

Thea stood among them, still motionless, still without having cast any magic of her own. As I moved closer, I realized it was because she was incanting. Her lips formed around whispered words as she stared sightlessly, far beyond the battlefield, as if addressing something – or someone – that we couldn't see.

A black, shaggy creature tore past me, roaring and growling. I yelped and leapt backwards. Sterling threw his hand over my chest, pushing me back.

"Stay out of Gil's way. It takes more effort for him to distinguish friend from foe when he's like this. I can heal out of it if he slashes me by accident, but you?"

"Got it," I said, eyeing Gil carefully. He was unstoppable when he went full dog, the term we casually tossed around the Boneyard to describe his full transformation into a lycanthrope. It sounded cute, but was ultimately completely inappropriate considering the carnage he wrought each time he entered the wolf state. "I have to deal with Thea," I continued. "She's planning something, but I don't know what."

"No. We'll deal with Thea." Sterling pushed me again as he gracefully dodged a tumble of limbs and tentacles – a shrike and a homunculus locked in mortal battle, ripping each other to pieces. "The others have this under control. We need to stop her before she completes her ritual."

We threw ourselves at Thea, raining down an assault from either side, me striking with Vanitas, and Sterling raking at her with his claws. Though making no sound, Thea's lips continued to move with increasing speed, her eyes calculating the angles of our blows. She whirled in place as she incanted, her hands lifting to erect shields of blazing light, deflecting both blade and talon with unearthly precision.

Sterling, with his preternatural reflexes, found an opening between the shields somehow. He slashed, and Thea faltered, three lines of black blood blooming on her torso. She looked down at herself, momentarily stunned, but recovered quickly enough to conjure a spear of light, her teeth bared in anger.

"Sterling," I shouted. "Get out of the – "

Thea was always fast. The spear left her hand, soaring like a rocket, slamming into Sterling's chest and throwing him off his feet. He screamed, clutching at the beam of solid light piercing his torso, struggling.

At least he wasn't dead. That was the only consolation. Maybe Thea missed his heart. But this was my opportunity. I slashed Vanitas in a wide arc, aiming for her head. Thea lifted her hand again, her fingers supporting a shield crafted magically out of solid light.

I twisted my strike at the last moment, catching her at the wrist.

The slash severed her hand. I watched with dark satisfaction as it landed in the grass at her feet, fingers twitching, talons raking at the earth. Thea screamed, her eyes widening at the stream of thick, black blood dripping from the stump that was once her arm.

Then she locked eyes with me. Her horror turned into glee, and her screams warped into piercing laughter.

Chapter 28

I looked on in revulsion as the meat of Thea's stump began to move. Sinew and muscle wriggled like little black worms, knitting and stitching even as she laughed. Bones erupted in slivers from the weaves of her ebony flesh, providing structure for her fingers.

Thea raised her hand in my face as a perfect layer of alabaster skin formed over it. Every finger looked pristine. New.

"What have you done to yourself, Thea? What are you now?"

She smiled, her fangs glinting in the starlight. "Better. Stronger. More powerful than you can possibly imagine."

"This isn't power, Thea. It's madness. The Eldest will warp you the way they warp all of their servants."

She laughed even louder, raising her talons to stroke at her cheek, as if both appraising and displaying her beauty. "I am not warped, Dustin Graves. I am a thing perfected."

"No. You're just insane."

"Insane? What is insane, Dustin, is forfeiting a portion of your freedom in exchange for something that is dead." Her eye fell upon my hand, upon Vanitas. "You bargained with a demon prince to bring back this weathered relic? How sentimental of you."

"You're one to talk. You're still on your ridiculous crusade to bring back your children."

I thought I caught the flash of anger in Thea's face, but when she spoke again, her voice was even thicker with mockery.

"That seems entirely reasonable to me, Dustin. What wouldn't you give to bring your loved ones back? Your family?"

My blood ran cold as her lips curved into a smile.

"What wouldn't you give to bring back your mother?"

The battle whirled around us. We were the eye of the cyclone, but every passing second, every word Thea spoke only stirred the storm in my heart. The Dark Room banged against its door. One thought, and I could kill her.

"She always did have a fascination for occult novelties, for strange antiques, your mother. All I did was sell her a box of trinkets. It was a simple matter of experimentation. With so much star-metal near her, I wondered, would the corruption take? Would her mortal body become fused with the energies of the Eldest?"

"You poisoned her. No human can take being close to that much corruption. We thought it was cancer. You killed my mother." I gritted my teeth, my vision blurring with tears, my palm stinging as I gripped Vanitas's hilt harder and harder. "Is that why you sacrificed me? Is that why you put your dagger in my heart, to test if I was the right subject for your insane plan?"

"Oh, it would have been glorious. If only you'd stuck it out with me, Dustin. If only the gem I placed around your throat could have truly controlled your mind. Imagine, me, an avatar of the Eldest themselves, and you, their greatest warrior, a thing that walks in the skin of a man, driven by the very darkest forces of the universe."

"I'm not your plaything, Thea. I don't belong to the Eldest. I don't belong to you. I can fight what you've made me. I won't turn into the monster that you are."

She tilted her head. "Oh. Is that so? These brothers of yours, the homunculi. I could see through their eyes, every step of the way. And I saw the look on your face when you killed the homunculus in the forest. The one that attacked your father." Thea smiled, her teeth glinting like daggers. "I saw the satisfaction in your eyes when you snuffed the life out of something that wore your face. Don't you feel it, Dustin? The thrill of murder. The sheer joy of taking something in your hand, and crushing it until it starts bleeding. Until it stops breathing."

But she was right. The urge to kill had become more and more difficult to resist, and my impulse to hurt and to slaughter had only grown stronger since the day I'd awakened to my powers. But I could control that. I was human, I told myself. I was Dustin Graves, a mage, a shadowcrafter. Someone's son.

"I'm nothing like you," I muttered.

"No. Of course not. And fortunately, for the sake of my experiment, you were nothing like your mother, either."

"Don't talk about her. I'll fucking kill you. I swear I'll – "

Sterling leapt out of the darkness in a flurry of fangs and claws, his fingers extended as they reached for Thea. She held up one hand – and caught him by the throat.

"Dust," Sterling shouted. "Whatever you're going to do, do it now."

But Thea – Thea had always been fast.

A gout of yellow brilliance roared out of her palm. This wasn't one of her light spears, not one of the weapons she could summon out of thin air. It was warm, familiar, bright. Sunlight. She'd shot him, point blank, with a massive burst of sunlight. Sterling screamed, and screamed.

The tattered remains of his body – the tangles of bone that still had his flesh clinging to them – rattled as they fell to the ground. Half of his skin, muscle, and organs had been charred into cinders. His face remained miraculously intact, but not much else was. His eyes stared glassily at the moon, his mouth open, unmoving. Something icy gripped its fingers around my heart.

"Sterling. No. You killed him."

"Undead filth," Thea said, dusting off her hands.

"No more," I shouted. "No more deaths. This is over."

Thea spread her hands. "Then end it, if you can."

I screamed as I charged at her, my heart thick with fury, my blood singing for vengeance. Vanitas's hilt grew warm and slick in my hand. Blood. The Dark Room had come before I'd even thought to summon it. Bursting from the ground, twelve black spears of solid night pierced Thea's body. She gasped, but did not falter.

"You tried that once before and didn't kill me, Dustin. End it. End it, you pitiful coward."

With both hands I raised Vanitas over my shoulder, rearing back with all the strength I needed to puncture Thea's armor. And with a great roar I thrust the sword forward, watching with berserk relish as the blade pierced her chitin, then sank into her flesh, searching through her chest. When Vanitas met her heart, I felt it beat. I felt it tremble.

Thea gasped, her head thrown back. Black blood trickled from the corner of her mouth. I pushed. Harder, and harder, until I knew that Vanitas had penetrated Thea from stem to stern. The compound eyes of an insect stared at me, passive, yet analytical. I stared back, unable to comprehend the alien insanity of the woman that was once Thea Morgana. The pillar of light above us wavered, then vanished. The shrike attack was finished.

"Your last words, Thea," I whispered. "Say them now. It's over."

Her eyes rolled down to stare me full in the face. "Do you remember," she croaked, "when I used your blood to commune with the Eldest? When I told you that I needed your blood at its sweetest, the fruit of your talent at its ripest?"

I scowled, then twisted the blade harder. She choked. "What are you talking about?"

"One of our first lessons at the Lorica, Dustin. A communion must always come with an offering."

Thea's gaze fell to the ground. The pile of artifacts the homunculi stole. Wasn't that her offering? But there they were, planted in the earth among the relics and trinkets. I don't know how I hadn't noticed them before: two gravestones, small ones, that might have belonged to children.

My blood ran cold.

Thea wrapped her hands around Vanitas, her fingers pulling the verdigris sword deeper and deeper into her body. She trembled, grimacing in agony, and she lifted her mouth to the witnessing stars, the blood trickling down her chin.

"I offer myself to the Eldest."

Chapter 29

Vanitas, the verdigris daggers, the chest of horrors left behind by my mother. All this time Thea was only waiting for her powers to grow, for her connection to the Eldest to mature, to make herself the greatest sacrifice there was. For how better could a priest of the Eldest serve her masters than by surrendering her very existence?

I don't know when Thea decided to give up on capturing me again and using my blood for her rituals. I don't know how she discovered that the watered-down blood of my homunculi was rich enough for inscribing the circle, yet not enough to offer as sacrifice. All I knew was that the heavens were screaming, twin beams of light lancing through the stars and the sky, each of them seeking one of the little gravestones on the hill.

Thea released Vanitas, then toppled backwards, the sword slipping out of her torso as she fell. She slumped to the ground, motionless. I felt no triumph, no satisfaction. We'd slain one threat, but all I had truly done was complete her ritual for her.

The shrikes had vanished, but so had the homunculi. The grass was thick with smears of blood, both black and red. Across the hill, Asher was sprawled on all fours, retching from the vast expenditure of his power. From somewhere behind me I could hear Carver calling my name. But above it all, what I really heard was the wailing.

Two voices, screaming, howling, from beneath the earth. Two children. The ground rumbled.

I ran for it.

"Dustin, to my side," Carver yelled. You can bet I dashed straight for him. Whatever was happening, an entire localized earthquake – and the horrific subterranean shrieking? Not good omens at all. "Steel yourselves. The worst is still to come."

But I wondered if we even had any fight left between us. Asher was still bent double, drenched in cold sweat. Gil remained in his wolf form, crouched by the edge of the hill, snarling and growling at something the rest of us couldn't see. And Sterling – God but I know that it's callous, but it was best for me not to think of what had happened to Sterling just then. We needed everything we had to fight. There was no time for grieving.

The little gravestones tumbled over, and the earth of the hilltop split apart, scarring as the first set of massive white talons burst from out of the ground. Each talon was the size of a human forearm, all of them sprouting from limbs as thick as telephone poles.

My mouth parched, I looked on in horror as more of those limbs erupted from the earth, scattering the soil as they lifted their bearers out of their graves, their bodies bulbous and fleshy, glistening in some awful, slick fluid. Two of these creatures, each the size of a small truck, finally freed themselves from their former homes. Each had the body of a huge, writhing maggot. Each raked its spear-like claws and long, spindly arms at the air.

And each bore the head of a young, long-dead child.

"Her children," Carver muttered. "She finally did it. She brought them back to life."

And at what cost? This was exactly as Bastion told me all that time ago, and exactly as Carver predicted. The Eldest have no loyalty, no understanding of mercy or human emotion, and even the wishes granted to their servants would be corrupted, perverted beyond recognition.

The two abominations, one with the head of a boy, the other, a girl, shrieked and wailed, both from their human mouths and from the multitude of tooth-lined gashes ripped into their heaving bodies.

"My babies."

I didn't think that Thea had survived. Yet with twelve gaping holes in her body, and a thirteenth punched through her heart, she was still moving, crawling on her hands and knees towards the bellowing monstrosities that were once her own offspring.

They turned to her with unseeing eyes, the heads of the two children bowing as they spotted the woman writhing in a pool of her own blood. But they turned away again, uncaring, showing no signs of recognition, no memory of the thing that was once their mother.

"My babies," Thea croaked, and something within my chest twisted.

I detested the very thought of feeling any sympathy for the woman who had murdered not just me, but my mother. Yet my heart still seized with foreboding when another beam of light slammed into the earth, only feet away from Thea's ragged body.

"No," she said, her head swinging from her children, to the pillar, and back again. "Please, no," she wailed, pleading to some unseen force. "I've only just brought them back. Time." She staggered to her feet, clutching at the holes in her belly, loping for her corrupted brood. "Please. Give me time."

A single black tentacle the size of a tree ripped out of the pillar of light, tearing through the veil between realities with a deafening crack.

Not this, I thought. The last thing we needed was another monstrosity to fight.

But the thing hadn't come for us. Thea's eyes went wide as the tentacle shot straight for her body. She screamed as it curled around her waist, dragging her towards the gateway. Her talons tore into the earth, digging great furrows as she fought to stay in our world, as she fought to be with her children once more.

"No," she screamed. "Please. No."

I'd never heard Thea so frightened. I'd never heard anyone so terrified. Her screams pealed through the night as the tentacle dragged her through the rift. The beam of light winked out into nothing, and just like that, Thea Morgana was gone.

But there was still the matter of her children.

Another howl tore through the graveyard, and before we could even think to coordinate, Gil had already raced across the hill, launching himself at the closest of the abominations. He was a roaring missile, jaws gnashing and frothing – but I couldn't even begin to think where he could attack the beasts and hope to slow them down, much less stop them.

He smashed into the monster, tearing at its belly with his claws. The beast reared back, lifted its own spindly, spear-like talons, and struck. Gil yelped like a kicked dog, stumbling into the earth, his fur matted and slick. Blood dripped from the awful gashes carved across his chest.

"Fuck," I said, raking at my hair. "Oh, fuck. Gil, oh fuck."

Carver tugged on my shoulder. "Dustin. The artifacts."

That's right. I'd forgotten about them, the entire pile still littering the ground between the gravestones. But the abominations had set their eyes upon us, and were moving with an awful, unholy speed, wriggling like great worms across the grass.

Worse, they were growing. God, but I hadn't imagined it. By some horrible twist the Eldest had given these monsters a form of cellular acceleration. It had started slowly enough, but between climbing out of the earth and attacking Gil, each of Thea's children had nearly doubled in size. Who knew how large they could become? And if they set their sights on Valero –

"We need to stop them. They're getting bigger, Carver."

"That hasn't escaped my notice. It will take most of my energy, but I should be able to trigger a detonation using the arcane power stored within the stolen artifacts. I'll need your help in this, Dustin."

"Okay," I stammered, forcing myself to calm down. "Okay. What do you need me to do?"

"I'll need you to shadowstep among the

children, to distract them while I work."

"Come again? I think I misheard you there."

"You heard me right the first time," he growled. "And I'll need you to hold them in place. Use your blades, the way you would pin insects to a board."

Or the way I'd done so with Amaterasu, and with Thea that same night. Use my blades like an iron maiden. That part? No sweat. I just needed to bleed half my body out to get the job done. The thing about distracting the beasts, though?

"Do it," Carver snarled.

I had no choice. We were the only ones left standing, and if I had to act as the decoy, then so be it. I walked into the shadows, traversing through the Dark Room. The mists were even more excitable, as if being used twice in the same night hadn't been enough for them.

They tumbled in the darkness, snaking tentacles and shadowy fingers over my skin, my cheeks. I might have imagined it, but it felt as if one of the tendrils reached for the wetness in my wounded palm, between my fingers, lapping at my blood.

I emerged in the graveyard, putting the pile of artifacts between myself and the pair of abominations. The smell of freshly turned earth grew thick in my lungs as I breathed. "Over here," I shouted, whirling Vanitas over my head as I did, his garnets and tarnished gold flashing in the night.

Thea's children howled as they caught sight of me, their human faces contorting into deranged masks of both hunger and hate, the dozens of mouths in their bodies baying for my blood. Slobbering and slithering, they wriggled towards me, towards the artifacts. Not one of them noticed when their bulbous, gelatinous bodies consumed their own gravestones as they approached.

I didn't hesitate. I slammed my palm into the earth, driving my intention into the shadows, to bring forth enough blades and spikes and spears to hold Thea's children in place. And this time I didn't need to cut myself open, either.

The Dark Room did that work for me, claiming its payment through the wounds that opened across my skin, in particular the one that ripped open over my heart. I grimaced against the pain, chuckling from deep in my throat. If Asher and Carver didn't have anything left over to heal me after this was said and done, I hoped that they'd at least have the strength to bury me.

Massive thorns of gleaming shadow tore through the earth, dozens of them conjured by my blood from the bowels of the Dark Room. The abominations shrieked as hooks and knives of solid darkness ripped into their flesh, a pit of spikes meant to seal them.

Drawing on the last of my power – and, I figured, the last of my blood – I sank into the earth, entering the Dark Room once more. With flagging strength I stumbled through its shadows, then reentered our world, falling onto my knees by Carver's feet.

He was still chanting when I reappeared, his hands shuddering as he summoned every trace of magic still left within his body. The sound of broken glass tinkled under the hideous screams of the wounded abominations – three, four, five of Carver's gems had fractured and cracked under the horrible weight of his spell. He thrust his hands forward, and with the roaring of a dragon a massive gout of pale fire shot through the night, hurtling directly for the pile of stolen relics. I held my breath.

The night shattered. The abominations howled. A prism of searing color exploded between the children, every artifact splintered and sundered by the might of Carver's magic. The torrent of arcane energy reached into the sky, blasting everything around them into worthless smithereens. Fuck the Veil, man. Hell, fuck the planet. If the normals knew where to look, and who to blame, this was practically a declaration of war.

The back of my brain ached from the brilliance, and I shielded my eyes until it faded. I only dared to look when the radiance had cleared. But there was nothing left on the hill. The combined detonation of the artifacts had obliterated the abominations thoroughly, disintegrating them down to the last atom.

Carver fell to his knees, his palms pushing against the grass. I looked around us, at the devastation Thea's final ritual had wrought. The hill had been cratered by the explosion, a perfect concave hollow carved into the earth. Diaz's body was somewhere on its slope, but from where I knelt, I could still see him breathing. Considering what Thea had done to his family, I didn't know whether death would have been more merciful.

Asher was still watching the hillside with his mouth hanging open, his face and neck glazed in sweat. Gil groaned, sprawled on his back across the wet grass, his chest torn open, but I knew he'd live. He just needed a half dozen raw steaks. That was all.

As for Sterling – there was no easy way to tell. At least half his body had been incinerated by sunlight, the rest of him only spared by the last minute twist he'd made to dodge Thea's spell. I stared in silence at his scorched body, hating that I couldn't tell if he was alive. He'd sacrificed himself to give me an opening to kill Thea.

And finally, she was dead. And yet, for the first time in a long while, I felt a swell of pity, of remorse. These creatures had been changed by the Eldest, but they were still children after all, innocents yanked harshly from beyond the grave by the misguided love of a grieving mother.

I couldn't believe it myself, but some part of me was uttering a silent, secret prayer for the Morganas. Perhaps Thea's one, small mercy was being spared the indignity of having to watch her own children die again. That I was still capable of having that thought told me that maybe – just maybe – I still had enough of my humanity to cling to.

But there would be time to think on that later. Sirens were wailing in the distance, because as far out of Valero as the graveyard was, the destruction of the artifacts had caused an explosion loud enough to alert the entire county. I was surprised that the Lorica hadn't shown up yet. The best part was that we had no evidence to show that this wasn't our fault.

I licked my lips to wet them, grimacing when I tasted the blood that had dripped into the corner of my mouth. "Carver," I croaked. "We have to go."

He lifted his head back, panting, his eyes squeezed shut. "Fuck the Eldest. Fuck the normals, fuck the Lorica, fuck all the rest of them." He chuckled bitterly. "The things we do to save the world."

Carver raised his hand to the sky, chanting. Ropes of amber fire reached out to the bruised and bloodied members of the Boneyard. One of them snaked around Diaz's unconscious body.

"Home," Carver cried, siphoning the very last of his power.

I gripped Vanitas in both hands, sighing as the flames of the sending spell consumed us. Home. The sweetest word.

Chapter 30

The Lorica did show up, I found out later on. They beat the authorities to it, which I suppose shouldn't have been a surprise considering how fast their teleporters could work. A few of the Wings escorted a Scion to the hilltop, who then threw up a massive glamour to disguise, if only temporarily, the fact that a fight had ever happened there.

Herald told me that it took some elementally-specialized Hands the better part of the night to dump enough earth to reshape the place, and even longer for the Lorica's cleanup team to get rid of all the shrike and homunculus viscera. At least it worked well enough to keep the normals in the dark.

What I learned in my early days at the Lorica

always lingered. How would the normals react if they knew we existed? What would they do if they realized that humans infused with the power of nuclear bombs walked among them in broad daylight?

Fortunately, at least when it came to my father, it wasn't all that much of a deterrent. It took far less work than I expected to include him in my life again. The first order of business was to give up the crappy house he'd taken up outside town. I helped him settle into a smaller place in Valero. It wasn't quite suburban swanky, but it felt good knowing he was closer by. I didn't mind funneling a chunk of my earnings into supporting him while he got back on his feet.

The best part was how quickly Norman got along with my coworkers. It took a little bit of time to convince him that Gil didn't go around sporadically turning into a rampaging werewolf, and that Asher wouldn't accidentally raise the dead in his sleep and kill us all. But after a couple of sessions at Mama Rosa's with a few beers, he started to see the Boneyard as I did: as colleagues, as humans, as friends.

But I didn't tell him about mom. He didn't have to know about how Thea had poisoned her with a box of relics. That I decided to keep to myself.

It was nice to see dad happy again, and to know that he'd resolved to control his drinking. A few light beers never hurt anyone, and I always made sure to throw him in a car or drop him off myself, just to be certain. I watched as he and Gil squabbled amicably over sports. Tonight, I thought, maybe I'll make an exception.

We'd found a great spot out on the sand, over at Lucero Beach. It was a nice evening, with good weather, and Carver had previously mentioned the possibility of us all going out for a proper little beachside barbecue, just the boys from the Boneyard.

Asher had latched onto that offhand remark for days, watching his weather apps like a hawk, waiting for the perfect opportunity to strike. And so it did, so we packed up and filed out to the beach, just a lich, a necromancer, a werewolf, a shadow beast, and his dad, a whole bunch of the undead and undead-adjacent, out for a casual nighttime barbecue by the ocean. No big deal.

"Look at this thing," Asher called out, plodding up from the surf with a starfish in his hands.

Carver raised a finger. "Put that back. And don't swim so far out. It's dark."

Here's your gentle reminder that Asher was eighteen. Sheltered, yes, but eighteen. Carver really was so overprotective of his favorite. I laughed. "It's not going to kill him, you know."

"Well and good, but that starfish belongs in the water. Put it back, Asher."

"Sorry," Asher muttered. "I got excited. Never seen one of these up close."

He hadn't seen a lot of things, and we needed

to keep that in mind for the future. It was so odd, knowing that this surging fount of necromantic power, this supernatural double-edged blade that could both kill and create was housed in the body of an earnest and slightly awkward young man. And maybe that was for the best. I slept better at night knowing that Asher had a curious, but gentle disposition. He was just a good guy in general.

"It's dark out, Mayhew," Sterling shouted. "You drown and I'm not swimming out to retrieve your sorry ass."

He exhaled a puff of cigarette smoke, somehow managing to do it angrily. Asher blubbered something indistinct but possibly very rude from among the waves. Sterling gave him the finger and laughed.

He'd survived, thanks in no small part to Asher's effort. And it wasn't the healing aspect of his necromantic magic that did the trick, either. Asher offered himself to Sterling as soon as Carver had teleported us from Latham's Cross to the Boneyard. Like, actually offered himself, letting Sterling take as much of his blood as he needed to rejuvenate himself.

It wasn't as much as I'd thought, as it turned out, but we did have to pull them apart once Sterling had regained enough of his strength. The hunger tied into how drained a vampire was, and as rare as Asher's power was, that made his blood an even rarer delicacy, an even tastier treat in the moment, which made it harder for Sterling to stop drinking. In not so many words, Carver, Gil, and I had to apply the arcane equivalent of a crowbar to rip Sterling off of Asher's wrist.

I thanked Sterling myself later that night, after his blood frenzy had faded. We couldn't have defeated Thea if he hadn't thrown himself directly at her. He shrugged it off and tried to play it cool, but I caught the beginnings of a smile in the corner of his mouth. Sterling could be an ass sometimes, but there was no way I could ever doubt his loyalty again.

Carver explained to me how we were all that Sterling had left, that immortality had ensured that anyone he liked or loved was long dead. We were his tribe, and as I saw at the graveyard on the hill, Sterling would do everything in his power to keep us safe. We were his family.

Diaz was offered room and board at the Boneyard, to at least give him time to sort out what he was going to do next. Carver said that we could always use a blood witch, but I knew him well enough to say that he extended his invitation out of empathy. Whatever else Carver had done in his long life, he was working hard to undo it. No one lost more than Diaz did the night the homunculi destroyed Nirvana, and while he was grateful for the offer, it was clear that he needed time alone. Last we heard, he'd left Valero.

"Dust." My dad waved a beer at me, beckoning me over. "What're you standing all alone over there for? Come here."

Gil was already sifting through a cooler, pushed into the sand alongside an incredibly cumbersome collection of jars and plastic tubs. He and dad had bonded over their mutual love of meat. As a werewolf, Gil knew his steaks inside and out, raw or otherwise, and dad had always been the type who could appreciate a good rack of ribs. I made a mental note to invite Herald out for one of these barbecues at some point in the future, then a second note to ask him to replace the jar of rub he'd used to cast his wards over dad's old house.

Vanitas was plunged halfway into the sand, his place of honor by the barbecue pit. He hadn't spoken yet, which naturally meant that he hadn't shown signs of moving, either, but I remembered how much he liked to be around people when there was food. Somehow he could taste it, or so he claimed. It didn't matter that his presence deafened me with his continued silence. It was just good to have him around.

"Fire's gonna take a while to get going," Gil said over his shoulder. "Might as well start it now."

I stuck my hands into my hips and scoffed. "Oh, please. I'll get it hot super fast. Just you watch."

Gil rose to his full height, dusting off his hands and folding his arms. He fixed me with an expectant grin. "Go ahead, hotshot."

I focused on my fingers, on my intention of setting the bundle of twigs and kindling and coal Gil had set up into a blazing fire. Hah, scratch that. I looked even further into the future. What I wanted was a nice, juicy burger, the exact damn thing that started off this ridiculous adventure in the first place. I wanted it flaming hot, better than anything that the Happy Cow could make. And I wanted it yesterday.

A spark of fire larger than I'd ever produced came bursting out of my fingertips. I bit back a yelp, and in my shock, flicked my wrist at the fire pit. The damn thing – a sphere of flame about the size of a golfball – launched from my hand and landed among the twigs. The entire mess burst into flames. A huge, roaring fire.

Dad laughed, pulling me in for a hug, then clapping me on the back. "That's my boy. That's my little pyromaniac." He pointed at me, practically jeering at Gil. "Hey. Hey Ramirez. That's my kid. That guy."

Gil shook his head and laughed. "Fine. I guess you're better at this than I thought."

I shrugged, playing it off like I'd meant for the fireball to happen, simultaneously tamping down the excitement of finally creating and shooting one on my own.

"See, that's what you get for not believing in me," I said, guffawing. "You just gotta trust in – "

But dad and Gil had already turned their attention back to their cooler, and to their shared range of grills and outdoor cookware that, I had to admit, confused me even more than the intricacies of the arcane. Ah, screw them. I made a fireball, and launched it all by myself. I mean I thought I was already at peak handsome, but I just got even hotter. Literally.

Like Herald once told me, like Hecate herself had once suggested, a step at a time. With practice and effort, I could still grow in power. Months ago I could barely create an ember. Who knew what waited next? Who knew what other possibilities lingered in my future? I almost wasn't bothered by the fact that I still owed a demon prince a favor. Almost.

But I didn't have the answers. As I looked around myself, as I breathed in the scent of the ocean and let the wind's fingers tousle my hair, I realized that I didn't need any answers at all. I chuckled to myself, somewhere deep in my chest. The waves crashed, and crested, and fell, echoing my laughter.

The men of the Boneyard drank blood, howled at the moon, raised the dead, and insane as it sounds, it finally felt like I belonged. I finally had what I wanted all along. I had brothers, my father, a family. And even for the space of just one evening, family was more than enough.

Need to read more?

Join Dustin Graves and his sentient sword Vanitas on an impromptu evening mission to stop a ritual sacrifice. Get your free copy of *Crystal Brawl* at **www.nazrinoor.com**.

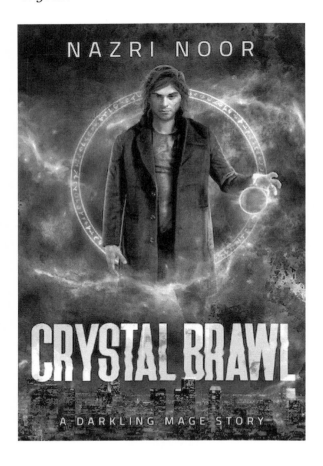

About the Author

Hi, I'm Nazri, a Filipino-Malaysian author based in California. I'm trilingual, but I really only write in English. I can also speak just enough Sindarin and Valyrian to impress absolutely no one. My urban fantasy novels focus on heroes who use wits, style, and their wildly unpredictable magic to save the day. Think sass and class, while kicking ass.

My influences come from horror and fantasy: HP Lovecraft, Anne Rice, George R.R. Martin, Chuck Palahniuk, Terry Pratchett, and Neil Gaiman. Growing up I was shaped by the *Blood Sword*, *Fighting Fantasy*, *Lone Wolf*, and *Grey Star* game book universes. I'm also inspired by video games, specifically the *Castlevania*, *Final Fantasy*, and *Persona* series.

Long story short, I'm a huge nerd, and the thrill of imagining wizards and monsters and worlds into existence is what makes me feel most alive. Writing, to me, is magic. If you enjoyed my work, please do consider leaving me a review. Thank you for reading, and thank you for supporting independent authors everywhere.

To see more of my books, follow me on social media, or simply say hello, visit me online at **www.nazrinoor.com**.

Made in the USA
Middletown, DE
17 November 2021

52760630R00172